Adventure in the Sierras

By HENRY R. FEA

Illustrated by HARVEY KIDDER

Ginn and Company

To MY PARENTS

ETHEL EDITH FEA AND HENRY FEA

Ginn Book-Length Stories
The Ginn Reading Program by David H. Russell and Others
Advisory Editor, Doris Gates

Home Office, Boston, Massachusetts 02117

Library of Congress Catalog Card Number: 67-15294

CONTENTS

DECEMBER

CHAPTER ONE

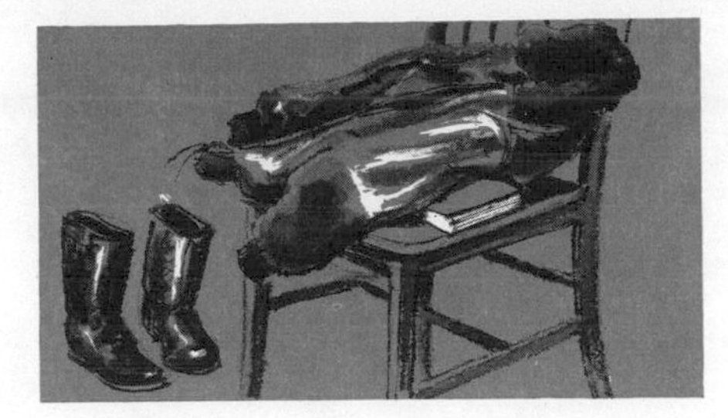

Taking Off

DAVID HAMILTON opened his eyes. The room was filled with the gray half-light which comes before sunrise. He looked at his watch. Six-thirty! Morning at last! He listened, holding his breath. There was no sound of rain on the windows. If it wasn't raining, Uncle Jack could take them to Denver today in the plane. David had never been up in an airplane.

In the growing light he could see his flying clothes on the chair—a pair of flying boots and a flying jacket. His mother had bought them for him for Christmas. In the coming dawn they looked man-sized. His mother was right, he thought; he was growing up.

There was something under the corner of the flying jacket. What? Then he remembered, and his eyebrows drew together in a frown. The book he was supposed to have been reading during the Christmas vacation! And last night his father had said that if David went to Denver the book went, too.

The flying jacket was of shining horsehide leather, black and so warm he was sure he would not feel cold in Denver, even though it was December and much colder there than here in San Francisco. There would be snow on the ground in Denver. His hand shot out to hold one of the flying boots. They were soft like Uncle Jack's. He drew the boot to him and smelled the leather. He would wear those boots to school when he got back.

School? David's eyes found the outline of the book again. He slid sideways under the blanket, letting one foot stretch out until the bare toes found the book on the chair. Slowly, now pushing one corner, now another, his toes guided the book across the chair toward the wastebasket. He couldn't practice reading the book in Denver if it didn't go to Denver, could he? When the book slid over the edge and fell with a clang into the wastebasket, David jerked back under the blankets and lay curled up, breathing in the warm darkness.

Suddenly he could not stay in bed another minute. He had to know for sure if they really were going to be able to fly to Denver. Throwing back the blankets, he jumped out of bed. His hand swept the curtains aside, and he looked out of the window. There was high fog, but there was no rain. "December twenty-seventh," he said, "and it isn't raining." He shivered and closed the window. Then he reached for his clothes.

As David dressed, he could hear the morning sounds of the house. There was the click of the switches on the electric stove, the solid thump of the refrigerator door, the clatter of dishes. His mother was getting breakfast. David pulled on his socks to keep warm.

His mind raced ahead. What if Uncle Jack let him fly the plane? What if they got lost in a snowstorm over the mountains? What if planes came out searching for them? What if—

"Fat chance," David said to himself. "Dad wouldn't let me fly a plane even if I knew how."

Parents never would let you do things because they were afraid you might get hurt. Growing up meant being able to take care of yourself—he knew that. And he was almost as big and strong as Dad now. He knew he could take care of himself.

Maybe today, though, after they had taken off from

the Oakland airport, Uncle Jack might let him take over the controls of the plane and head for Denver. His breath was tight in his chest as he thought about it. But Mother would probably speak to Uncle Jack before they left, and make him promise not to let David do anything like that. He stood in front of the mirror and yanked at his shirt, stuffing it down inside his jeans. He ran his hands through his black hair to make it lie down.

As David finished dressing, he heard a scratching at the kitchen door and a whining. That was Patty, the black-and-white cocker. David listened, hearing the outside door open and his mother's voice from the patio. "Well, Patty. Yes, you do love us, don't you?" His mother's voice grew stronger as she came back into the kitchen. "Go wake David. Go wake David, Patty! Go on!"

Then, as his mother's warm laughter floated to him, there came a scampering of feet and a small panting breath. A flurry of black-and-white dog burst through the half-open doorway and flung itself onto his bed.

David shouted with laughter. "Ha! Fooled you that time," he said. "Thought you'd catch me asleep." He jumped onto the bed and wrestled with Patty,

holding her down so that she growled and barked. She squirmed free and washed his face, her warm pink tongue darting in and out as he rolled to get out of the way.

"Morning!"

David recognized that booming voice from the kitchen. He slid off the bed and pulled his shirt straight. That was Uncle Jack's voice. If Uncle Jack was up, he wanted to get out there so he would not miss anything.

"Morning, Tom!" Uncle Jack's voice boomed again.

David heard his father's quiet answer, "Morning, Jack."

David started down the hall with Patty trotting along beside him. Everyone was up except Jeannie. David hesitated outside her bedroom door. Then he turned the knob quietly and let Patty inside. He shut the door again and walked quickly toward the kitchen. As he went through the kitchen door, he heard Jeannie shriek and Patty bark. Jeannie was a sleepyhead, and Patty loved to awaken her because Jeannie always made such a fuss.

Uncle Jack and David's father were in the breakfast nook. Uncle Jack looked up from his grapefruit as David appeared. A smile broke across his round face. "Well," he said, "thought you were never going to get up. Your father and I have been waiting breakfast for you for hours and hours. Nearly left for Denver without you."

"Oh! No!" David said. For a moment he believed Uncle Jack. Then he remembered Uncle Jack's tricks and laughed as he took his place at the table. "You haven't been up so long, either," he said. "I heard Mother come to the kitchen, and she's always the first up."

David looked across the table at his father. Dad said nothing, but he was smiling.

Then his mother's arm brushed his as she placed his grapefruit in front of him. He was glad she had not kissed him, as she usually did, but he was sorry too. He started to wonder why, but all at once he was hungry and dug his spoon deep into the grapefruit.

Uncle Jack was talking about the weather. "A little soupy, but it should be good flying weather when we get above the fog," he said, "and bright and cold in Denver. Man! Does it get cold there!"

David watched his mother as she pulled the plug from the coffeepot. "You're perfectly sure it will be safe, Jack?" she wanted to know. Her gray eyes were serious.

Uncle Jack looked up suddenly. David knew his uncle had intended to laugh but something had changed his mind. "Sure, Mary," he said. "I wouldn't dream of taking them if it wasn't." He drank some of his coffee. "Oh, accidents do happen," he added, "but the plane is a safe little thing. I fly it all over the country. And we just have to fly across the Sacramento Valley, then over the Sierras and across Nevada. We'll be there long before dark."

David held his breath. He remembered times

before when his mother had looked as serious as she did now. She might decide not to let them go!

When his father spoke, it surprised David. Dad usually sat back and let Mother decide things like this. "All small birds have to fly sometime, Mary," Dad was saying. He was smiling a special smile that David knew was not for him or for Uncle Jack. It was for Mother and for her alone.

"There are roads all the way, and cars, and ski lodges in the mountains," Uncle Jack explained.

But Uncle Jack could have saved his breath, David realized. Mother had decided to let them go. Dad had done that.

"All right," his mother said. "I know you'll take care of them, Jack."

"I promise you that, Mary." Uncle Jack looked as serious as Mother.

David sighed with relief. It was settled. They could go!

Jeannie came into the kitchen with Patty growling and jumping around her.

"Well, sleepyhead." Uncle Jack reached out to pat Jeannie's blonde braids as she passed him. "Thought you had decided not to go with us."

"Of course I'm going!" Jeannie laughed. She went around the table to kiss her mother. "Morning, Mother," she said. Then she went around to her father and kissed him. Then she sat down in her place by Uncle Jack.

David wished now that he had kissed his mother. Before he could think about it, he felt Patty's cold little nose touch his hand under the table. It was not until after he had dropped a piece of bacon into Patty's mouth that he remembered his mother's firm

rule about feeding Patty at the table. Patty's jaws came together with such a snap on the bacon that David was sure his mother must have heard, but she gave no sign.

The grownups were talking further about the trip, and David could hardly eat his breakfast he was so excited. He wondered why Jeannie seemed so calm. Maybe girls did not get excited about plane rides. Perhaps, when you were only ten like Jeannie, you did not realize how important it was. Perhaps.

"You'll reach Denver tonight, that is, December twenty-seventh," his mother said. "You have to be back here by the second of January. That will work out just fine because school begins on the fourth." She got more bacon for Uncle Jack while she talked. "They have warm clothing for the snow, Jack, and I know they are going to love your ranch in winter. They have never seen it at this time of year."

Uncle Jack beamed. "Bet they'll find it different," he said. "A ranch does look different in winter. Even the cowboys look cold."

"Be sure to give my love to Ethel," Mother continued, "and don't let David do anything dangerous."

"Oh, oh," David thought. "Why did parents

always have to think you were going to do something they did not want you to?"

When his father and Uncle Jack left the table, David followed them to the den. He wanted to see what his uncle had bought to take back to Denver.

When David entered the den, his father had a rifle in his hands. The light from the lamp gleamed on the blue steel barrel, and the stock was slick and shining.

David held his breath. "Could I hold it a minute?" he asked.

His father smiled and handed it over to him. The rifle felt light but heavy, fragile but powerful, and feeling it made David so excited that he stuttered. "W-w-w-what kind is it?"

"The name and caliber are on the barrel close to the stock," his father told him.

David swung it around quickly and stared at the numbers and letters. The figures were .30-.30. The old helpless feeling came over him as soon as he looked at the letters. W-I-N, he saw. "*Win*" he thought; then the rest of the letters came fast one after another so that they swam together—CHESTER. David gripped the barrel hard in his hands. He did not want his uncle to know that he had trouble reading. Uncle Jack was such a wonderful person! He flew a plane and he shot with a rifle, and—

"It's a Winchester, David," his father was saying, and smiled at him.

David's hands loosened on the rifle. "Yes, a Winchester," he said. The pause had been slight; Uncle Jack would not guess. "A Winchester," David said again, then, "Do you suppose—"

His father was smiling as he interrupted, saying, "Yes, I'd not be a bit surprised if he might let you." He and Uncle Jack looked at each other. "After you get out on his ranch where there are no people around, and after you learn how to handle a rifle, you may try out this one." His father's eyes were stern suddenly. David found that he had tipped up the rifle and was pointing it at Uncle Jack.

David lowered the rifle quickly and carefully. "I'm sorry," he said.

Uncle Jack was collecting his purchases. "And the skis and ski poles," he said. "Five pairs this time for my new foreman's family, and the rifle for Bill, one of my cowhands. Here are a few other things I picked up yesterday." He turned over a large first-aid kit and some other things that David did not bother to identify. "Good bargains here," he continued, "especially right after Christmas. Well!" He looked at his watch. "We should be leaving if we're going to get to the ranch before dark."

David ran to his room for his flying jacket. He could hear the men carrying things out to the car. His fingers were clumsy with the zipper, as he tried to hurry. He ran down the hall for Jeannie. He found her in her room in front of the mirror, looking at herself in her new red ski suit. "Girls," he thought. "Come on!" he burst out.

Jeannie swung around to face him. "What's the matter?" she asked.

"Nothing!" he said. He carried Jeannie's bag down the hall to the garage.

Somehow people and bags and supplies managed to get together beside the car. When everything was packed, Father and Uncle Jack got in the front seat. David, Mother, and Jeannie got in the back.

"You know," his mother said, as the car swept downtown and across the Bay Bridge, "I'm going to miss you two around here." Jeannie snuggled up beside her mother. David let his mother's hand rest on his

shoulder. Take-off time was coming close now, and he wished that Mother and Dad were going, too.

Dad was not saying anything as he sat beside Uncle Jack, but he caught David's eye in the rear-view mirror and winked.

"Your Uncle Jack is the best pilot I know," Mother said, "and your dad is the best car driver I know." Her arms tightened on Jeannie and David. "And David is going to be just as good a driver when the time comes for him to get his license," she added.

David just had time to realize that perhaps his mother did plan to have him grow up someday, to drive a car, maybe even an airplane, when they reached the Oakland airport. Now things began to happen so fast that David had trouble sorting them all out. Then he was leaving Mother and Dad, and Jeannie was holding tightly to his hand as they went through a side door and out onto a strip. Uncle Jack's plane was there, sitting all alone in the wisps of morning fog. There was a mechanic working on it.

As they approached the plane, the mechanic looked up from his work. "Hi! Mr. Milton," he shouted.

"Hi!" Uncle Jack shouted back. Then he turned to David and Jeannie. "Up and aboard!" he said.

David found himself climbing into the small plane with Jeannie still holding tightly to his hand. They took the back seat, sitting side by side on the long cushion. They watched the men load the baggage and supplies.

It was warm in the plane, but David felt Jeannie shiver. Her blue eyes looked enormous against her white face, her mouth serious above her red collar. "I'm afraid, David," she said.

David tried to laugh but his voice squeaked. He

forced himself to lean back in the seat. "I guess it's because we haven't been up in a plane before," he said. "Don't worry. I'll take care of you." The words were out before he thought, and he looked at Jeannie, expecting to see her laughing at him.

"I know you will, David." Her mouth curved up in a smile, and David felt her relax. "I'm silly."

"No, you're not." David suddenly felt wonderful. Jeannie thought he could do anything, really anything. He looked out.

Uncle Jack put the last pair of skis and an axe into the baggage compartment, then threw in a roll of blankets, picked up a big covered basket, and shook hands with the mechanic. Why the basket? Then David remembered that it was the one they always took on picnics. Mother must have filled it with food for them to eat on the way. He breathed deeply, all the way down into his chest. They were going to be up in the sky in about three minutes now. He knew something wonderful was going to happen.

CHAPTER TWO

Down in the Snow

THE LOW THROB of the engine built up to a roar, and the little plane shook. The airport, his mother and father outside, the flapping windsock—all seemed unreal, shaking like the television screen when it wasn't tuned properly. Everything was blurred, and the world was a world of sound. David could not get his breath and was but dimly aware of his uncle adjusting levers, turning switches.

"Fasten your safety belts," Uncle Jack said over his shoulder. There was a rushing sound. The earth slid away under them. Then they were climbing into the sun above the wisps of fog, and the airport was falling away, falling down. Suddenly all feeling of motion stopped; there was just the noise—the noise and the tight feeling in David's chest.

Uncle Jack sat back in his seat, shrugged his shoulders, and smiled around at them. "Scared?" he shouted.

"No!" David shouted back, and he found that he could breathe. Of course he had been—well, just a little worried, but he was sure he had not been afraid. It had been hard to breathe for a while; that was all.

"Oh-h-h-h!" Jeannie let go of David's hand as she shouted. "I was," she said. "I was really scared." She laughed, and her nose wrinkled because she laughed and smiled at the same time. She bounced up and down in her seat. "This is fun."

David rubbed the hand that Jeannie had gripped. She had held on so tightly that it was stiff. He had not noticed it when they were taking off. He sat back and smiled, too. "Boy!" he said. "Boy!"

David was getting used to the noise. Flying was not exactly what he had imagined it would be. He had not expected the roar. But, of course, a plane could not fly without an engine, and an engine had to make noise. He noticed that his uncle was looking over his shoulder and pointing down. The plane was circling the Oakland airport.

Far below lay the long, thin ribbon of runway which

they had left, and the windsock that showed which way the wind was blowing. And the fog! It hung along the hills and down across the water to San Francisco, so that the Golden Gate Bridge stood deep in mist with only the tops of the high pillars showing above the fog bank.

Oakland looked like a picture in his geography book, labeled "Oakland, California, from the Air." So this was what it meant! He would understand when he looked at that page again. David did not like to think about his geography book. It was difficult to read, and it wasn't a bit exciting. He would look up that picture again, though, when he got back to school, to see if it really did look like this.

"David!" Jeannie pulled at his jacket as she called to him. "David, look!"

He crowded close to Jeannie and leaned forward to see what his uncle was showing her. It was a map of California unfolded on his knees. "Here," Uncle Jack said, pointing with his finger, "here is where we are." His finger moved from Oakland, tracing a line to the right across the map. "We're going this way."

"That's east," David said.

"That's right." Uncle Jack's finger moved along.

"Across Stockton, toward Nevada." His finger moved up. "Here's Lake Tahoe. We fly south of it but might be able to see it if it isn't foggy in the mountains."

"Oh!" Jeannie was bouncing up and down in the seat again. "We will see the mountains, won't we Uncle Jack?"

"The Sierra Nevada Mountains," David said. He could hear his teacher saying, "Now in the eastern part of California, and dividing our state from Nevada, lie the Sierra Nevada Mountains, usually called the Sierras."

"They are usually called the Sierras." Uncle Jack said the same thing.

It was hard to hear with so much noise. Jeannie was still bouncing up and down. David felt he would like to bounce, too, but that would look childish. It was warm in the plane, warm and noisy, and there was no feeling of motion. It was as though they were not going anywhere. David leaned forward again toward Uncle Jack. "How fast are we going?" he asked.

Uncle Jack's finger showed him on the air-speed indicator. David read the number under the needle. "Ninety," he said. "Ninety miles an hour."

All at once the mountains rose out of a cloud bank before them. Still, solemn, and white they stood in the brilliant sunshine. In a long line they stretched away to the north, marching on and on in their cloaks of white snow, with dark patches of shadow on them. The shadows might be patches of trees, or cloud shadows, or bare black rock.

"Wouldn't it be fun to land and play in the snow?" Jeannie asked.

"No!" Uncle Jack laughed. "It would be difficult to land there at all," he said. "The snow is very deep in the mountains this time of the year, and only a few people live there. It would be very dangerous. They might never find us."

There was no talk for a little while, and David thought about what Uncle Jack had said. He watched the mountains marching away to the north, cold and frightening. No, he decided, it would be much better not to land there. It would be much better to go safely over the mountains with their deep snows and their loneliness.

"We'll have to go higher soon," Uncle Jack was saying, "to get over the mountains. It will be colder in here then. Let's see." He looked at his watch. "Getting on toward eleven. Perhaps we should have a sandwich."

At the thought of food David was hungry. "Yes," he said, "let's."

Jeannie opened the basket. "Ham or turkey?" she asked.

They sounded so good David could hardly wait until Uncle Jack had chosen. Then he could wait no longer. "Ham," he said. "No, turkey—no, ham!"

Jeannie laughed. She handed him two sandwiches, one of each kind.

"Thank you," David said. He took a very large bite of ham sandwich and let it slide back on his tongue until he could taste every bit of the delicious ham with mustard. "Ham sandwiches are the best," he said.

There was no answer. Uncle Jack and Jeannie both had their mouths full.

David ate his ham sandwich, then his turkey sandwich. Then he started on another ham sandwich. He watched the instruments on the panel and Uncle Jack's hand on the levers. How he wished that he could be flying this plane, that it would change course to his hand as it did to Uncle Jack's! He thought about a question for some time before he asked it. Perhaps Uncle Jack would laugh at him, but he had to ask. "How long will it be before I can fly a plane?"

Uncle Jack did not laugh. He adjusted one of the knobs so that the engine changed its sound a little. "You can take lessons and get your pilot's license when you're seventeen," he said.

"That's a long time," David thought. It seemed forever. "I think I could learn to fly now," he said.

He expected Uncle Jack to laugh at that, but he

didn't. He turned and looked right at David with eyes gray like Mother's. "You probably could," he said. "It isn't that a younger boy couldn't learn to fly a plane. It's that we don't know what he would do with a plane if we let him." He turned back to the knob and went on fussing with it.

Uncle Jack was right, of course. David admitted to himself that he had been thinking, if he could fly, he would fly around the schoolhouse so the boys could see him, and that would not be a very smart thing to do. "I wish I were seventeen now," he said. "I wish I were."

Uncle Jack was still fussing with the knob. "Stop wishing your life away," he said. "There are lots of things you will want to do before you are seventeen. You will be grown up soon enough. And it isn't all fun." He seemed to get the knob set to suit him. "Some day you will find it's happened," he said, "and then you won't be too happy that it has." He reached back to pull Jeannie's braids. "Do you want to grow up right away, too?" he teased her.

"Yes," she said. "I want to be a dancer and wear long dresses."

"I give up," Uncle Jack said. Then he sat forward

in his seat. "We are going to go higher now, what pilots call going upstairs," he said. "We have to be a bit higher to cross the mountains. We are high enough now to get over them, but mountains cause air currents that blow up and across in strange ways, and they make down drafts which drop the plane suddenly quite a few feet. So we fly high enough to keep out of trouble," he finished.

David heard the engine take on a new sound, and the plane tipped up. It seemed as if they went up a very little way; then Uncle Jack leveled the plane again. "That's enough, I think," he said.

The mountains had been getting closer. To David it did not seem as if he were going toward the mountains, but as if the mountains were coming slowly toward him. The outline of separate mountains was clear now, with deep blue valleys between them, and harsh black pieces of rock that stood out against the blue sky above the fog. Sometimes there were openings in the fog, and David could see flat, smooth white places that must have been meadows or lakes.

"Might just as well see what's going on in the world," Uncle Jack said. He turned a button, and the radio came on.

"I didn't know you had a radio up here," Jeannie said. She was surprised, and it surprised David a little, too, although he had thought he recognized a radio dial among the other dials and instruments.

"Yes," Uncle Jack said, "all the comforts of home." He laughed. "With you two and my radio and that big basket of sandwiches, I'm snug as a bug in a rug."

David was wondering how Uncle Jack's radio could work up here without electric power; then he thought he had the answer. "The radio—" he said, "it works on a battery like a car radio, doesn't it?"

"Uh-huh," Uncle Jack said. "That's right."

The radio came on with a blare. "And now," the announcer was saying, "we bring you a little girl about whom you are going to hear great things some day. Yes, we give you—"

David did not listen. The radio was always saying it was giving people things, great things, and all it did was let girls sing. It would be much better if they had really great people come on the programs, like football players and great pilots, like—

David knew something was wrong. The engine noise had changed, and Uncle Jack had snapped off the radio and was staring at the instruments, his jaw hard along the side of his cheek. The sound of the engine continued to change. It seemed to cough, then hesitate; then it coughed again. Uncle Jack's eyes darted over the dials. He fiddled with several knobs.

Jeannie's hand found David's, and he took it in his. He had that feeling again about finding it hard to breathe, about a weight on his chest. Outside, the sun shone cold and lonely on the miles and miles of rolling fog. Ahead the mountains rose, cold and lonely, marching away to the north. Inside the plane it was warm, and there was the pleasant smell of ham sandwiches still in the air, but there was also a waiting feeling in the plane, and there was the quiet. The propeller kept turning, but there was no sound from the engine.

David's voice was loud in the silence. "What's wrong, Uncle Jack?" he wanted to know. Jeannie gripped his hand tightly.

Uncle Jack did not take his eyes from the instruments, and his voice was slow, as though his mind was on other things. "Nothing to worry about, I think. We might have a wee bit of ice in the carburetor." He continued to study the dials.

Jeannie was huddled close to David and she whispered, low so Uncle Jack wouldn't hear, "Are we going to crash, David?"

David's voice was loud to cover the worry he felt. "No, silly," he said. He started to laugh at her; then he saw the worry in her eyes. "We're going to be all right," he said. "Aren't we, Uncle Jack?"

There was no answer from Uncle Jack. He was busy pulling the heat-control knob, adjusting it, then changing it. David found himself counting, "One . . . two . . . three. . . ." The plane had nosed down slightly; they were losing height.

Slowly the minutes ticked by. Uncle Jack worked, his hands going quickly from throttle to heat-control. A cord stood out on the back of his neck, and it throbbed so that David could see it move. There was perspiration on his uncle's forehead, too. "Seventeen . . . eighteen . . . nineteen . . . twenty," David counted. The silence was strange and lonely, and the plane creaked. There seemed to be so many little sounds that had been covered by the noise of the engine. David heard Uncle Jack breathing, and his own foot scraping on the cabin floor. His breath came out in a long, slow sigh, and he looked at Jeannie. Her face was white and her eyes were enormous. "I'm scared, David," she whispered.

David realized that the engine was not going to start again. Uncle Jack stopped working on the levers and closed one valve securely. "I shut off the gas," he said. "I hope when we get down lower the fog isn't too thick, and I can pick a soft place for us to land. There are a number of little lakes around here. I know Silver Lake can't be so very far from where we are. The snow is about six feet deep now, so we should be able to land without too much of a crash if the plane doesn't nose over. It all depends on whether I can get enough time and space between the fog and the mountains. Be sure your safety belt is tight, David, and check Jeannie's."

Uncle Jack turned and was looking at David and Jeannie. "Put your jacket up over your head, David. Jeannie, you do the same." Then he turned back to the controls.

David held very tightly to Jeannie. There was no sound except for the sigh of the wind in the wings. Then they were in the fog and drifting lower . . . lower . . . lower. Through a fold in his jacket David saw trees and snow, then fog . . . then trees and snow . . .

more fog. Then he saw Uncle Jack straighten up in his seat and turn a lever very fast. The plane banked around and there was a whistling sound underneath as it touched the snow. The whistle grew to a wild rushing sound as the plane went forward into the snow. Then came a splitting crash. . . . Silence. . . .

David found himself sitting sideways in the seat, having been wrenched around. Jeannie was huddled

at the other end of the seat, crying. There was a smell of dust, and the plane was tilted forward at a crazy angle. Then David heard Uncle Jack groan. He reached for the buckle of his own safety belt. He slid down to Uncle Jack. "Are you all right, Uncle Jack?" he asked.

"Get Jeannie unfastened," Uncle Jack shouted. And David found himself scrambling up the inclined floor and reaching for Jeannie's safety belt. Grown-ups never allowed you to think for yourself. He had just wanted to make sure. Uncle Jack spoke as David slid down to him again. "That's good. See if you can get me out of here. I think my leg is broken."

CHAPTER THREE

It's up to David

DAVID would never forget the few minutes after the plane crashed. The noise of the crash was followed by layer on layer of quiet like a thick blanket. There was only the quiet, and the settling dust, and the tilted plane.

He held the broken seat where Uncle Jack had sat. Jeannie held the other side of the seat. Uncle Jack lay between the broken seat and the broken instrument panel. It was one of those times that should have gone away so that he could laugh and forget it. But it couldn't go away because it was real. His hands trembled on the broken seat.

Jeannie spoke now. "What are we going to do, Uncle Jack?" she asked. "Will anyone find us?"

David looked from Jeannie to his uncle lying against the instrument panel. Uncle Jack's leg was folded queerly under him so that it stuck out at the wrong angle. David felt a little sick when he saw it. His heart pounded inside his chest and seemed to be echoing Jeannie's words. "What are we going to do?" it said. "What are we going to do?"

David wanted to stay there holding to the broken seat until his uncle's voice told them that everything was going to be all right. But he knew Uncle Jack couldn't tell them that, for everything wasn't all right. Uncle Jack couldn't do anything with his leg folded under like that. David knew it was up to him to do something. Now, for the first time in his life, a grownup couldn't help him. Now it was up to him, David.

He moved along the broken seat, not letting go of it because his legs shook. He reached Jeannie. "Everything's going to be O.K., Jeannie," he told her. He patted her shoulder. Together they climbed around the broken seat and crouched down beside the injured man. David noticed how dark his uncle's eyes were, almost black, and Uncle Jack's hand gripped part of the broken instrument panel so hard that the muscle bulged under his coat. There were great drops of perspiration standing out on his forehead.

"This old leg," Uncle Jack said. "Are you hurt, Jeannie?"

Jeannie felt herself in several places. "No," she said. She felt more places. "I guess I'm all right," she said. "Does your head hurt, David?"

"No!" David was surprised. "Why should it?"

"There's a big lump." Jeannie's hand came up to his forehead. "There."

It hurt when she touched it, but David shook his head. "It's O.K.," he said. Now he knew why his head throbbed.

"I think you hit it on my elbow," Jeannie told him, making a face and rubbing her elbow carefully. "Ouch!" she said.

Uncle Jack was trying to move away from the instrument panel. "If both of you are all right," he said, "you can help me get this leg of mine in shape." He groaned as he moved, and David saw that he had his teeth set. "Don't you worry," he said, as inch by inch he moved himself into the open. "The three of us are going to be just fine. We'll get along just fine.

His breath came in gasps. David wondered why he didn't stop talking. "The plane will stay warm for a while, perhaps long enough for you two to get some splints on my leg. Then we'll look around and see if there isn't a summer cabin on this lake, where there is a good stove. We need a place to stay for tonight."

Jeannie's eyes widened. "Won't we get rescued before tonight?" she asked.

David held his breath, longing to hear that they would—knowing that they couldn't. When the words came they were what he expected.

"I'm afraid not," Uncle Jack answered. "Not tonight, Jeannie, but a plane will come over tomorrow for sure." He lay still on the floor of the plane. "Listen, David, and you too, Jeannie. My leg has to be put in splints. You are old enough to make a good nurse, Jeannie, and David is going to show you what to do so you can help him. I may faint when you start," he warned them, "or I might yell, but you go right ahead putting on splints. It has to be done. Perhaps I can get a little farther out into—"

David saw that his uncle's eyes were closed and that his head had fallen to the floor of the plane, and he knew that the pain had been too much.

"Uncle Jack! Uncle Jack!" Jeannie called as he made no move. Her voice rose.

"We better do what he says," David told her.

"But we don't know how," Jeannie said.

"Yes, we do," David was surprised to hear himself say. He pulled her to her feet. "There's a book on first aid with the other things Uncle Jack packed in the plane. Here, I think we can get it without opening the door and letting the cold in." He pointed to the space behind the seat where Jeannie and he had sat. "There, between the roof and the back of our seat—that piece of leather. I think it unfastens, so we can get at the supplies from here."

As David talked, he pulled the snaps on the leather. The leather flaps came away, and David put his head and shoulders into the opening. In the dim light he could see the supplies, jumbled from the crash. He had to find that book, but his head was aching again. The rifle was there, and several boxes of ammunition. "Here are the skis," he called over his shoulder, and passed a pair out to Jeannie.

"We'll need skis and poles," he told her. "The snow's deep. Uncle Jack said so." He turned over the roll of blankets, matches, some cans of food, an axe. "Here," he said suddenly, as his hand felt the smooth box. He pulled it from among the supplies and drew his head and shoulders out of the opening. He turned and handed the box to Jeannie.

They opened it together. "These are bandages," Jeannie said, "and a bottle of iodine."

David's hand darted into the box and came out with the first-aid book. "Here it is," he said. He handed the small black book to Jeannie. "Read what it says," he told her.

Jeannie held the book on her lap, and David looked at the cover. He had not minded giving her the book because Jeannie never teased him about his weakness in reading. He stared hard at the words on the cover. First there was an *E* and then a small *m* and several syllables he couldn't make out. Then there was the word *Kit;* he could read that. Then there were two long words, much too long for him. He looked at Jeannie.

Her troubled eyes met his. "I don't know either, David," she said. "It's too hard." Then her eyes lighted. "Maybe we can read the part about fixing Uncle Jack's leg, though. Let's look in the index." She handed the little book to him.

David flipped through the pages, but his heart was heavy. He knew he never could do anything if there were directions that had to be read. He found the index, and his finger moved slowly down the list of words. "I can't find *Broken*," he said when his finger had reached the end of the *B's*.

"I remember," Jeannie said. "Our teacher told us it comes under *Fractures*." Gently but firmly she took the book from his hands.

"You read what it says, and I'll do it." David assured her.

"David!" There was worry in Jeannie's voice. "There are some big words here, too. I hope—"

David was hoping, too. They couldn't let Uncle Jack down when he needed them. They just couldn't! He scrambled back to the opening above the seat. "I know we need two splints, anyway," he said. "We can use a pair of ski poles. I can cut the ends off with the axe, or if they won't do, perhaps I can split a ski."

He pulled out the smallest pair of skis, then the ski poles, jerking at them, pulling out the axe, making his muscles work so that he couldn't think about the worry in his mind. Sooner or later, when the splints were

ready, they were going to have to put them on Uncle Jack's leg. David didn't know how, and they couldn't read the book. He worked as fast as his hands could move, until his breath came short and he could feel drops of perspiration on his head. Then he heard Jeannie's voice behind him.

"He's awake," Jeannie was saying. "Uncle Jack's awake!"

David turned to see Jeannie on her knees stroking Uncle Jack's head. With a *whoosh* David let all the

air out of his lungs and slid down to them. Uncle Jack was very pale. He groaned and turned, gritting his teeth. But he was awake.

David spoke quickly for fear his uncle might faint again. "Tell us what to do." He bent down over his uncle. "How do we get the splints onto your leg?"

Uncle Jack groaned while they waited. It seemed as though he had not heard David. Then the words came slowly, between his tightly set teeth. "Cut away . . . the leg of my slacks. . . . Don't move my leg when you do that. . . . Then cut the boot laces and get the boot off." David got out his knife and followed the directions, moving carefully. "Now get one of those small blankets from the back of the plane. . . . Get something for splints . . . and some belt lacing . . ."

When David came back with the things, Uncle Jack looked paler than before. "Lay the blanket out flat beside my leg. . . . Then straighten out the leg." David saw that his eyes were dark with pain. "Pull my leg *straight* . . . and *don't bend* it after that, no matter what else you do. . . . Get the blanket under and around it . . . and the two splints tight alongside the blanket. Wrap the leather lacing around the leg . . . and around the splints so they won't move."

It seemed easy once they started. Jeannie held the leg out straight while David got the blanket under and around it. His hands trembled, but he worked as fast as he could and as carefully. He put ski poles for splints on each side of the leg. Then David tied leather lacing around each splint and around the blanket so that the splints would not slip. Uncle Jack had fainted again. David tied the last piece of leather in place and sat back on his heels.

"We did it!" He smiled at Jeannie and saw the answering smile in her eyes.

Jeannie placed her hand gently on the wrapped leg. "Poor Uncle Jack," she said. "He was so brave. It must have hurt him very much."

David turned his mind to the next job. "I'm going out," he said, scrambling up to the door.

"Hadn't we better stay here?" Jeannie watched him as he pushed at the door. The door frame was twisted from the crash, and the door wouldn't open.

"We can't just stay here," David said. "Uncle Jack can't do anything, and it will get freezing cold here. The heaters won't work now the engine is stopped."

He found the axe among the things he had pulled out of the baggage compartment. Then he put the blade of the axe into the crack between the door and the door frame and pried at the door. Jeannie came to help him, and they both pushed at the handle of the axe. Slowly, with metal grinding on metal, the door opened. There was a rush of cold air; then they were kneeling in the doorway looking out.

The snow lay deep, in huge blue-white banks among the fir trees, and in long blue-white swells across the frozen surface of Silver Lake.

Jeannie shivered. It was very cold and very quiet, so quiet that she whispered, "What are we going to do now?"

David looked far across to the dark green pines on the other side of the silent lake. Then his eyes followed the jagged line of mountains around to a point of land which stuck out from the lake shore. "I don't know," he said.

It was a white world, white and still, with a low

gray sky over it all. "See the marks in the snow. The plane must have curved as it hit the ice—" his arm pointed to show Jeannie as he talked— "and it swung in here under the trees. The plane is down deep in the snow now. We'll have to get the skis and start looking for a cabin, I guess."

"Won't we be rescued today, David? Won't somebody send a plane for us?" Jeannie asked.

David watched his breath as it hung in a cloud in the still, cold air. How he wished he could tell Jeannie that a plane would come! "I don't know," he said.

Jeannie shivered and drew back into the plane. "Shut the door, please, David," she said. She put her hand on his arm and whispered again, "I'm scared. Aren't you?" She did not wait for his answer but slid down the floor.

David watched her bend over Uncle Jack. He ran his tongue around his lips so they would not feel so dry. "Uncle Jack said there are hunters' cabins around the lake," he said. "I'm going to get the skis and try to find one."

"There might be a hunter's cabin right behind the point," he told himself as he sorted out the skis and chose a pair for himself. The hunter would know what to do for Uncle Jack, and he would have food and a warm cabin, and he would get in touch with Oakland.

David was glad that Jeannie and he had learned to ski during their week-end trips to the mountains. His flying jacket would keep him warm, and he had his gloves. Then he saw the rifle and pulled it out.

Jeannie saw the rifle in his hands as he turned. Her eyes were big. "David," she said, "you mustn't take that."

There was comfort in the feel of the heavy polished stock, and in the sight of the long blue barrel. David had been having a little daydream about meeting a hunter, and the hunter knowing that if David carried a rifle he must be grown up. The hunter would say, "Hi, Pardner—" Then Jeannie had interrupted the dream.

He did not know how to use a rifle. And his father had told him that a rifle in the hands of a man who does not know how to use it is a very dangerous thing. "I'm not taking it," David said angrily. He put down the rifle and picked up the axe. The axe would be better than nothing.

With the axe in his hand he stepped to the door. He wished his father were with him.

Jeannie scrambled up beside him. "I'm coming with you," she told him. Her eyes were large and afraid, and her mouth was set.

David wanted her with him, but he looked at his uncle. "We mustn't both go. You stay with Uncle Jack," he said. "I'll be right back."

Jeannie looked at Uncle Jack, then back at David. The fear was still in her eyes, but she turned back toward Uncle Jack. "I'll stay," she promised David.

David dropped the skis onto the snow and lowered himself until his feet found them, taking care that he did not fall and sink into the deep drifts. Jeannie came again to the doorway, watching him fasten the ski bindings. He tried a few slides, then waved back at her. "Close the door," he said. "Take care of Uncle Jack."

The door closed with a grinding thud, and David was alone in the white world. He had never felt quite so alone in his life. The skis moved steadily under him in the smooth slides that his father had taught him, taking him out onto the surface of the lake. He fastened the axe to his belt and headed straight for the point of dark firs that hid the end of the lake from his view.

The snow was very deep. He must be careful not to fall, he told himself. It would be difficult to get up again. Skiing was hard work. He stopped to listen, but there was no sound but his own breathing. He held his breath and thought he could hear his own heart beating in the stillness.

He wanted to turn back, but the thought of his father made him keep the skis moving along, leaving two unsteady tracks on the lonely snow-covered surface of the lake. "Yes," his father would have said, "there isn't anything else to do, David. Your uncle is hurt and Jeannie isn't very old. It's up to you to do something about this whole thing."

"I know, Dad," David found himself thinking, "but I don't know what to do and I'm scared." He kept the skis going steadily. "It's all right for you," David found himself arguing with his father, "because you know how to use a rifle if there was a bear or something, but you never taught me how to use one. I know I could handle a rifle if—"

He finally reached the point of firs. He could see now it was a thin finger of land sticking out into the

lake, and he could almost see through the trees to the opposite shore. He moved faster in spite of his heavy breathing, reached the end of the point, and stood still in the cold air, his breath coming out like puffs of smoke. Then he saw the cabins.

There were three cabins. One was quite near, then another about a mile farther along the shore of the lake, then a third a long way up the lake shore. His heart sank as his eyes searched the cabins for a sign of life. The snow seemed trackless; there was no sign of smoke from any chimney. Perhaps, he thought, it would be better if he went back to the plane and asked Uncle Jack what to do next. The cabins looked lonely and frightening. Then he thought of his father again. His father would have said, "What would a man do in your position, David?"

David's hand touched the axe at his belt, then he started forward again toward the closest cabin. It must be about two in the afternoon; Dad would be in his office, Mother safe at home. The cabin was quite near now. It was built of logs, close to the shore of the lake, with snow piled in great drifts around it and against its walls, and its windows boarded up. In front of it there was a short landing pier for boats.

He slowed his pace and moved quietly, listening between breaths, watching the boarded windows, the drifted-in door, the roof piled high with snow. Then he looked back at the dark green point which now hid the plane from his sight. He skied toward the cabin. There was a large padlock on the door. "I couldn't open it with that lock on there," he said to himself.

"Yes, you could," his father seemed to be saying to him.

"I can't break into a house. It's against the law," David thought. But he found himself feeling the strong steel head of the axe with his hand and knowing that the law did not hold when people were in trouble and really needed help.

He skied up beside the pier, slipped the skis off his feet, and turned them around so that they were headed back toward the point and the airplane. Then he moved away from them, wading along the pier slowly, hating to leave them, listening, watching. Nothing moved; there was no sound. He reached the door, listened for a long time, hating to break the silence. Then he raised the axe and chopped at the hasp of the padlock.

The cabin was dark inside. The air had a dead feel and a cold, musty smell. He stood in the doorway with one foot inside so he could see around the door into the cabin, and one foot outside so he could run if something came. He did not know what the "something" might be, because he did not want to think about it. "If anything makes so much as a squeak," he thought, "I'll be out of here and back to the plane so fast the skis won't even touch the ground. They won't leave a track at all."

As his eyes became used to the dim light from the cracks between the boards over the windows, he saw the whole inside of the cabin. It was a large square room opening out from the doorway where David stood. At his left the wall went straight up to the sloping roof. There was a huge stone fireplace in the middle of that wall. It was big enough, he judged, for him to walk into. Opposite the doorway was a blank wall of rough boards. He looked to the right, to the side of the room opposite the fireplace.

There was a platform ten feet high, with cots on top of it and a rough stairway leading up to it. Below the platform was the kitchen, consisting of cupboards, a sink, and an iron cookstove. There were benches and a rough board table in the kitchen part of the cabin, and big chairs and fur robes around the fireplace.

David backed out and swung the door shut. He tried not to think as he hurried into the skis and started toward the plane. "Maybe someone has come to the plane by now," he wished, moving out onto the lake and glancing back sometimes over his shoulder at the dark cabin. "Maybe Uncle Jack will find out his leg is just sprained, and it will be all right by the time I get back," he told himself. "Maybe Dad—"

David knew it wasn't any good pretending. No one would have come to the plane. Uncle Jack's leg was broken. Somehow he was going to have to get Uncle Jack and Jeannie to the cabin, because there was no stove in the plane. David moved slowly across the frozen lake. The sky was dull gray, and a few flakes drifted down.

"It's not fair," he thought. "It's getting dark, and it might snow, and I don't think I can look after Jeannie and Uncle Jack all by myself." A tear worked its way down his cheek and then another. "And I guess I'm afraid, too," he said aloud. It was a long way to the airplane, and he was tired.

Jeannie was waiting in the doorway of the plane. "Is there a cabin, David?" she called.

He saved his breath until he reached the plane.

"Is there, David?" She was huddled in the doorway, her jacket collar pulled up around her face. "I'm cold," she said. "It must be freezing in here now."

"There's a cabin," he told her as he unfastened the ski bindings, balancing with one hand against the side of the plane so that he would not sink into the deep snow. "But there's no one there, and it's cold, too." He was about to tell her that he did not know what to do but he saw how worried she was. "We'll manage," he said, not knowing how.

"How, David? What are we going to do?"

Things didn't seem so bad now that he was back at the plane with Jeannie and Uncle Jack. He realized how lonely it would have been if he had been all alone on this lake. "Yes," he said again, "we'll manage somehow." He climbed through the doorway into the plane. "There's a stove in the cabin," he told her, "and wood beside it. We can light a fire in the fireplace too."

Jeannie's eyes searched his face. "How are we going to get Uncle Jack to the cabin?" she asked.

David opened his mouth to say he didn't know; then he got the idea. "I think," he said, "we could make a sled out of some of those skis." He smiled as he went on, seeing the plan form in his own mind. "And if we both wear skis, we could pull him across the lake to the cabin."

"David!" Jeannie's face was shining, even though she shivered again with the cold. "I knew you'd think of something," she said. "And Uncle Jack's awake now. Maybe he could help, too, to get himself onto a sled. He's pretty heavy for us."

Uncle Jack lay where he had been when David left. His leg, wrapped in its blankets and splints, looked like a giant cocoon. Jeannie knelt beside him and patted his hand as she told him of David's plan to get them to the cabin, while David watched them and sat down to get his breath. "We're going to make a sled for you," Jeannie assured Uncle Jack.

"We'll nail the floorboards of the plane across a pair of skis," David added.

There was silence. Uncle Jack frowned, then spoke. "The floor boards are almost impossible to get out of these little planes," he said. "You would have to take out too many of the pedals and other machine parts first, or chop the boards up, and then they wouldn't be much use for anything."

Jeannie shivered. "I guess we'll have to stay here," she said.

"We can't do that," David said. "It'll get too cold." There was surely something he could use for boards to make a sled, even though most of the plane was made of metal.

"David's right." Uncle Jack raised his head, and his voice was sharp. "David! I want you to get out another pair of skis for Jeannie. I want you both to get on skis and go to that cabin. Get a fire lighted and stay there where it's warm."

"What about you?" David stood up and looked back at his uncle.

"I'll be fine. This blanket will keep me warm. Tomorrow a plane will come."

"What are we going to do, David?" Jeannie turned to him.

David realized he must think of something. His eyes went around and around the plane, looking for anything that would make a sled. Uncle Jack couldn't be left here. He would die. Perhaps that's what Uncle Jack planned. The thought was so bad that David put out his hand to get hold of something solid. His hand touched the door.

"The doors!" David pounded one with his fist. "Uncle Jack, the doors!" he said. "The doors have wood around them. I can chop them off with the axe and nail them across two skis for runners!"

David rubbed his fist, bruised against the door, while he watched Uncle Jack's face. Then Uncle Jack smiled. It was a weak smile, but it was there in his eyes, and David felt relief warm in him right down to his toes.

"Why, sure!" Uncle Jack spoke to himself, thinking it over. "You could pry them off with the axe. They are just held to the frame by screws through the hinges." He rested a minute. "It might work," he said. "We don't have nails, but I think I know how it can be done." His smile was broad now. "Good for you, David!"

David got the axe and ran the blade down between frame and door hinge. He slipped the blade in the crack between the door and the frame and jerked at the axe handle. There was a splitting sound, and the

screws drew out of the wooden frame. They stayed in the loose hinge, hanging there with small bits of wood clinging to them.

"Uncle Jack won't fit on that door," Jeannie announced. "It's too small."

"We'll use both doors," Uncle Jack explained, while David moved the axe down to the lower hinge. "If we use one behind the other on two long skis, there will be room for me and for the supplies. Then if you two can pull me, we'll all get to that cabin yet." David was getting ready to spring the lower hinge. "Wait, David! Don't take the doors off until we think of some way to fasten them to the skis. It's going to get very cold, once the doors are off."

David sat back and closed the door. "If there aren't any nails," he said, "I can bang the screws through the doors into the skis with the axe."

"It won't work," Uncle Jack told him. "The skis would probably split, even if the screws were long enough. We'll have to use lacing, and tie the doors to the skis somehow," he said. "Get the skis out on the snow, and then help me pull myself up to the doorway. When I see you out with the skis, perhaps I can think of a way to fasten the doors on."

David felt as though he could lift the plane and carry the whole thing to the cabin. It was so wonderful to have Uncle Jack telling him what to do! "I'll get the skis out," he said. He opened the door, its loose hinge flapping, and pushed the longest skis from the baggage compartment out onto the snow. Then he threw out all the other skis and the ski poles too, and the leather lacing. He got onto his own skis and lined the two long skis up, headed toward the cabin. Then he tied the rope to the small iron step under the door, opened the door again, and threw in the rope. "Ready, Uncle Jack," he said.

Uncle Jack reached for the rope. His face was very pale, and his hands trembled as he took the rope; so David realized that the broken leg must be hurting him again. "Now if you will hold the door open, Jeannie," he said, "and if you will come in here, David, and get hold of my belt and give me a hand to heave myself along, I think maybe I can get to the doorway."

Taking off his skis, David climbed in to help as Uncle Jack pulled himself slowly, painfully along the floor. Jeannie stood by the door, biting her lips. "Please don't faint again, Uncle Jack," she kept saying to herself. "Please don't faint again."

Finally, inch by inch, minute by minute, they made it, and Uncle Jack lay in the doorway looking out and down at the two long skis. David covered him with a blanket, then pried off the two doors and got them outside. It was growing late, and David was tired and cold, but he felt that Uncle Jack was guiding him now.

Uncle Jack gave all the orders. "Get those laces. Chop a little hole in the upper corner of that door. Be careful, now! Don't chop too much—just a little hole so the lace can go through. Now tie the lace around that ski pole, now to the ski binding. There! Good boy, David."

And all the while that David's cold, tired, stiff fingers worked with the laces and the skis, the doors and the poles, he could hear orders for Jeannie too.

"That's good, Jeannie," Uncle Jack encouraged her. "Get over the seat into the baggage compartment. Now push the supplies out onto the back seat. That's right. Hurry, so we won't get too cold before we get out of here."

Jeannie's voice came to David as he worked. "Blankets," she said, "and matches . . . and a gun . . ."

"It's a rifle," David shouted.

"O.K. A rifle . . . a ham, woolen socks, a box. What's in the box?"

"Ammunition," Uncle Jack told her.

"Ammunition, more blankets . . . a can of food. . . ."

David could see the pile of supplies rising beside the doorway near Uncle Jack's head. Jeannie must

be out of the baggage compartment now. The supplies would be ready when the sled was finished. He straightened his tired back and groaned. The laces held the doors on securely now.

"Good boy, David." Uncle Jack's tired voice came to him. "We'll manage just fine with you two working like beavers, and me lying here like a lazy lump.

Jeannie, you're wonderful! Don't know any two I'd rather have a plane crash with. Once more, David, lace that pole to the tips of the skis and through a screw hole and through the hole you punched with the axe. If you don't, the skis will turn inward when you and Jeannie begin to pull."

At last the sled was finished, and they loaded the supplies. "There!" Uncle Jack said. "Good for you! Now to get me out of here. I think I can raise myself with your help, then lower myself through the doorway with my arms . . . if you and Jeannie can push the sled back under the doorway, and steady my legs when they come down. You will have to be *very careful* with the broken one." His hands reached under the blanket for the door frame. "Get on the other side, David, and give me a hand," he said.

Finally, slow minute by slow minute, they made it, and Uncle Jack lay on the sled, his head on the supplies, his eyes closed. They tucked the blankets around him. David and Jeannie got on their skis and took their places inside the rope ahead of the heavy sled.

"It's going to be pretty hard work," David said to Jeannie. He knew with the first pull. "It's going to take us a long time to get to that cabin, but I think we can do it."

"We've got to do it," Jeannie said, tugging at the rope.

It wasn't as lonely as crossing the lake by himself had been, David thought, but it was very hard work. They pulled together for a few steps; then they stopped to pant. Then another few steps, then another stop to pant. After a little while it seemed to David that they had been dragging the heavy sled for days. Each time they pulled it, the sled seemed heavier. Each time they traveled a shorter distance before they had to stop for a rest. Each time they stopped to rest, they had to stop longer.

Gradually the trees grew dimmer on the point behind them. Gradually the cabin loomed closer. Snow was falling, not enough to be called a snowstorm, but it made the day darker, and David saw that the afternoon had gone and that it was evening.

Just as he had given up hope of ever reaching the cabin, they made it. The sled was at the drifted pier, then up the pier to the doorway, and Uncle Jack was smiling weakly at them from his blankets as they sat panting on the doorstep.

"You two are just about the finest pair I ever met," Uncle Jack said. "Just wait until I tell your mother and dad about this."

"Oh!" Jeannie panted. "I thought that we would never, never, never make it. I thought we were going to be stuck out on the lake. I thought I was just going to fall down there in the snow and stay there, flat on my face." She looked at David as he sat on the steps with his chest heaving. "You're awfully strong," she said. "I guess that's the only way we made it."

"You pulled your share, too," David told her quickly. Jeannie's words meant a lot to him. Perhaps some day his father and mother would see that he had grown up. Jeannie knew he had.

"Now," David said as he heaved himself to his feet, "we'll haul one of the cot beds down from the sleeping loft in the cabin and make it up with rugs and blankets and then get you into it, Uncle Jack."

Jeannie made up the bed after David brought the blankets in and the robes down from the sleeping loft. "There," she said, "I think maybe I am a good nurse after all. Isn't it nice, David?"

David looked up from the hearth, where he was shaving some wood as his father had taught him.

"Yes," he said. "You'll make a good nurse. Now let's get Uncle Jack onto that bed."

Slowly, painfully, Uncle Jack was brought in. By pulling the sled right into the cabin and working all together, they got him onto the bed, and David lit the fire in the fireplace. He and Jeannie sat for a minute on the edge of Uncle Jack's bed, feeling the fire warm the cabin and its light make the gloomy room cheerful. But David knew they must not sit still long. "We have to get things ready for the night," he said, and he went to work, unpacking the sled and prying the boards off one of the windows.

Jeannie explored the kitchen. "There are lots of pots and pans and some dishes here—and some cans of food, David."

Uncle Jack looked as though the pain wasn't so bad now. "Jeannie, you will have to be a good cook as well as a nurse," he said; then, "Is there a woodpile, David?"

"I'll see," David told him and went outside to explore. From there he could hear Jeannie telling Uncle Jack, "There are some sandwiches left, and there is that ham you bought in Oakland, to take to Denver. There's a can of coffee here that hasn't been opened.

And there is some other food in cans. Where can we get water, Uncle Jack?"

David walked around the cabin on his skis, poking the axe into every big pile of snow to see what was under it. He found the woodpile at last. It was behind the cabin. He got the sled and loaded it with big logs. As he came around the cabin with his load of logs, he was surprised to see how dark it had grown. The lake had disappeared in the shadows, and the trees stood close, black and quiet. David hurried with the wood. Then he went inside with the first armful and met Jeannie coming out with a large kettle.

"I'm going to get it full of snow," she explained. "Uncle Jack says we'll have to melt snow for water. And I don't know how to light the fire in the kitchen stove," she added.

David carried in the wood and dumped it beside the stone fireplace. Then he took the lids off the kitchen stove and looked at the cold grate. He crumpled up some paper that had held sandwiches, put in a pile of the shavings he had not used in the fireplace, and struck a match. When he had added wood and the fire burned brightly, he put the lids

back and set the kettle full of snow on the stove. "There," he said, "that ought to do it."

He went back to the door to make sure it was closed tight. Then he used the axe across two cleats in the door to bar it so that nothing could get in.

Jeannie had been exploring in one of the cupboards. "Look, David," she called, holding up two cans. David knew they were cans of beans because the picture was on the label. "There are lots of cans of food here," Jeannie said. Her eyes were dancing and she seemed happy now. "But some are pushed out at the ends."

"The frost has done that," Uncle Jack called. "Those are spoiled. Don't use them. What else is there?" he asked.

Jeannie was on her knees, looking inside the cupboard. "Beans," she said, "and corn, and soup. And here's a can that says 'butter.' They don't can butter, do they?"

"This must be a hunter's cabin," Uncle Jack told them. "The hunters come up here in the fall to shoot deer and bear. They bring all sorts of things in cans."

"There's flour here," Jeannie continued. "Maybe I can bake something if Uncle Jack shows me how." She laughed. "This is fun!"

David sat down on one of the bear rugs. They had got Uncle Jack to the cabin, and it was nice and warm. "Pretty good for a boy," he thought, "pretty good." And he was sure they would be rescued by tomorrow. They would be fine here tonight. Yes, it was fun. He could smell the coffee that Jeannie was making, and they had plenty of sandwiches for tonight.

He looked around the cabin, at the dancing shadows the firelight threw on the walls—and then at the rifle leaning in the corner. He was sure they would not need it, but he was glad they had it. His eyes strayed to the dark shadows and then to the window where he had torn off the boards. Something soft was whispering against the blackness of the glass. Snowflakes! If it snowed very heavily, it would cover all traces of the plane and even the tracks they had made. David decided he would ask Uncle Jack, but seeing the deep hollows under his uncle's eyes and the way his face was drawn, he did not ask. He would keep that worry to himself until tomorrow—until tomorrow.

CHAPTER FOUR

A Day of Waiting

It was still gray when David awakened. He lay curled up in a ball with his legs tucked under his chin. He had gone to bed in his clothes under a pile of blankets, but the cold soaked through to him and he shivered. All about him in the coming light were the dim gray shapes of chairs and table, and above his bed was the gray blur of the east window that looked out across the lake.

For a moment he was puzzled; then the events of the day before rushed into his mind. He carefully felt his forehead. The bump was still there, but it wasn't so large and it didn't hurt much. He looked across the cabin. Uncle Jack was still asleep.

David raised his head so he could see Jeannie's bed over near the fireplace. Jeannie had rolled herself up in a ball, too, and she had pulled the blankets right over her head.

"December twenty-eighth," David thought. He clutched the blankets up around his ears to keep out the cold. "At home Mother always gets up first. I guess here it's going to be my job." There was no sound of cars, no Patty scratching to be let in, no sound of anything. David saw his breath like smoke when he breathed above the edge of the blanket into the cold air.

His mind went back to his mother and father in San Francisco. What would they be doing now? Probably they had been so worried that they had not gone to bed at all last night. Aunt Ethel would have phoned his mother as soon as the plane failed to arrive in Denver. Suddenly David was excited. Maybe their names would be broadcast over radio and television. Boy, he would have something to tell when he went back to school! Perhaps there would be airplanes out looking for them, even army planes. The announcer on the radio would say: "The plane was last seen. . . . Jack Milton and his niece and nephew,

Jeannie Hamilton and David Hamilton of this city. . . . It is not known. . . ."

Perhaps when they were rescued today, maybe—maybe they might even ask him, David, to say something over the radio. He would say— But if he did not get up, the rescuers might find him in bed, and he would not want that to get on the radio.

"If I get out fast without thinking about it, maybe it won't be so cold," David said to himself. "I'll count to ten, and then I'll jump out and pull on my flying boots and run over to the fireplace and get a fire going."

He looked at the dark fireplace with its small heap of gray ashes. "One—two—" he began to count. It wasn't very comfortable sleeping in all your clothes, but it was easy to get up when all you had to put on was boots. "Three—four—" He held his breath, getting ready to jump. At "ten" he threw back the blankets and dived for his boots. Teeth chattering, he got out his knife and went to the fireplace. His hands were stiff, and it was hard to whittle the wood shavings to start the fire.

He arranged the shavings, then pieces of small wood crisscross, then a heavy log at the back against the fireplace wall. He crumpled up a piece of newspaper from the wood basket, shoved it under the shavings, and took a match from a tin box on the mantel.

By the quick flash of the match David could tell that his uncle was awake. His head came up so that David saw his sleep-rumpled hair. "David?" he asked.

"Yes?" David said. "It's cold."

The flames licked at the shavings, moved to the light wood, and flicked up the fireplace wall. The wood began to crackle, and white smoke disappeared in a curl up the chimney. The firelight made dancing shadows on the cabin wall.

Uncle Jack pulled himself around in the bed so that he faced the fireplace. "Thought you were never going to wake up," he said.

"How is your leg?" David asked.

"Thought it would keep me awake, but it didn't." Uncle Jack stretched and yawned. "It hurts a little but not too much." He watched David stretching his hands out to the fire. "Did you hear the owls last night?" he asked.

"I don't think so." David was about to confess that perhaps he would not know an owl even if he heard one, when he realized that his uncle was laughing at him.

"Bet you didn't." Uncle Jack ran his hand through his unruly hair. "You and Jeannie were asleep last night before your heads hit the pillows."

Jeannie's head came out from under her blankets. "It's cold," she complained. "And it's awful to sleep in your clothes. I feel all wound up in stuff."

"You'll both feel better when the cabin gets warm and you have some breakfast," Uncle Jack said.

"When are they coming to rescue us?" Jeannie demanded.

"Well, I was right on course for Denver," Uncle Jack said. David relaxed as he heard the confidence in Uncle Jack's voice. "Planes flying over here should see the wreckage of our plane."

"Boy!" Jeannie smiled sleepily. "Wait until I tell my teacher all about us crashing and living in a cabin."

David lit the fire in the cookstove while Jeannie got out of bed, put her shoes on, and combed her hair. Uncle Jack punched two pillows down behind himself so that he could sit up and see what went on. Through the window David watched the coming day. The rising sun made a rose-pink light on the snow and the pines along the lake shore.

"Going to be a bright and sunshiny day." Uncle Jack's voice came from behind David. "Good flying weather. A plane should be able to find us easily."

David did not answer because he was back in the kitchen and had just made a dreadful discovery. It just couldn't be true, but it was. What did people do when they were away off by themselves like this in a cabin and discovered that they had no bread to eat? "Uncle Jack!" David held up the one sandwich left from the night before. "Look," he said.

"What's the matter?"

"This is all the bread we have." Staring at the small dry pieces of bread, curled at the edges and showing the ham inside, David felt hungrier than he had ever felt before in his life. He felt as though he could hold at least six loaves of bread, and there wasn't one.

Jeannie spoke out of the silence in the cabin. "I'm hungry."

"Surely you two didn't drag me all the way to this cabin just to starve me to death?"

David caught the twinkle in Uncle Jack's eye and sighed with relief. Uncle Jack must have an answer to the problem. "We can feed you beans." He laughed.

"I don't like beans for breakfast," Uncle Jack said. "Jeannie is just going to have to cook."

"I can't!" Jeannie looked from David to Uncle Jack and back to David.

"You'll have to," David told her. "We have to eat. But what could we cook even if Jeannie could cook?" he asked Uncle Jack.

"Pancakes."

David's mouth watered. "Sure," he said. "Uncle

Jack can tell us how, Jeannie." He turned back toward the cookstove.

Jeannie wore a puzzled frown. "I don't know," she said. "I guess we can try. What do we need?"

Uncle Jack named the articles, checking them off on his fingers as he did so. "Flour, salt, baking powder, butter, and milk—if there is some. It's a good recipe. I used to make pancakes before your Aunt Ethel and I were married. Now she does all the cooking."

David was down on his knees, looking through the cupboards. "Flour in this can." He pushed the can out and went on looking, his hands sorting the articles. "Salt—baking powder?" He could not see anything that looked like baking powder. "Butter, yes—in a can, and here is some canned milk," he called out.

Jeannie was looking, too, reading the labels. "Here's the baking powder," she said and gave it to David. "Everything seems to be here, Uncle Jack."

"Fine, fine!" Uncle Jack laughed. "We'll have pancakes and ham for breakfast. Get a mixing bowl and a frying pan, Jeannie."

David held the can of baking powder and studied the words. "B-A-K-I-N-G—P-O-W-D-E-R" he whispered to himself. He touched each of the letters with his finger. Why was it so easy for Jeannie and so hard for him?

While Jeannie mixed the pancakes, David went for wood. He was so hungry he could not wait around till the pancakes were ready. He put on his jacket and took the axe from the door.

The sun was rising over the mountains as David stepped out into the cold white world. Everywhere the snow sparkled in the sunlight, and everywhere it was quiet. There wasn't a breath of air or a sound to break the lonely brightness of the morning.

David pulled the collar of his jacket up around his ears and pushed through the new snow to the woodpile. With the axe he poked around in the snow for long logs for the fireplace. His breath came in clouds of steam, and his nose felt cold already. The logs were too big for the cookstove; so he set to work to split some of them.

The pile of split wood grew slowly, and David got warmer, but at last he was so hungry he could not split another log. He picked up an armful of the split wood and went back to the cabin. It was filled with the wonderful smell of cooking pancakes. Jeannie stood by the cookstove, her face red from the heat, her

hand tight around the handle of a huge pancake turner. "Boy," David said, "that smells good!"

"Told you Jeannie would make a good cook." Uncle Jack was sitting up against his pillows, watching Jeannie. "This will probably be the best breakfast you ever ate, David." Then he stopped talking, looked at the wood in David's arms, and asked with a frown, "Did it snow last night?"

"Yes." David dropped the wood into the wood basket as he spoke, brushing the new snow off his jacket. "It's pretty."

"Can you still see the tracks we made crossing the lake yesterday?" Uncle Jack tried to raise himself high enough to see out of the window.

"No," David said. "The new snow has covered them up. I guess—" He forgot what he was going to say because his uncle looked worried.

Uncle Jack wasn't really talking to anybody but himself when he spoke. "The plane—hard to see from the air anyway." Then he looked directly at David. "After breakfast," he said, "I wonder if you could get back to the plane and brush the snow off it. We want to make sure that when a plane flies over here looking for us, it can see our wrecked plane."

David was glad Uncle Jack had said *after* breakfast, because he was so hungry he did not know if he could make it without breakfast. "Sure," he said. "I'll go." Then he turned to Jeannie. "I'm so hungry I could eat the pan too."

Jeannie didn't laugh. She looked just the way Mother looked when she was not sure whether they were going to like what she had cooked. "I hope these are right," she said. And David knew what she was going to say next even before she said it. "Now, if we can just eat them while they're still hot—"

"I think," Uncle Jack said, "that David is about to break the record for eating pancakes."

The pancakes were good and they were hot, and David did eat so many of them that he surprised even himself. When he had finished, he grinned at Uncle Jack and patted his stomach. "Should take me all the way to the plane and back," he assured him. "You're a good cook, Jeannie, and I'm finally filled up to the top."

David fetched more logs and built up the fire before starting off. The skis moved quickly over the soft snow without a sound. He carried the axe, and his collar was turned up around his face to protect it from the cold. He reached the wooded point and rounded it. There was the plane, all right, just as they had left it yesterday under the trees. There was some new snow on it, but not as much as David had thought there would be. The branches above it had caught most of the new snow. The plane looked cold and lonely. David skied up to it and stood panting, his breath coming in long gasps. He slipped out of the ski bindings and pulled himself up and into the plane.

It seemed much colder inside the plane than outside, and it smelled of gasoline and of old engine grease. David climbed the sloping floor to check over the supplies once more. There might be something, he thought, which they could use—rope, tools. No more food here; no more blankets, either. His eyes darted around the plane. No, there wasn't anything else they could use in the cabin. He climbed down and went to the front of the plane. Taking hold of the broken propeller, he swung himself up to the top.

The metal surface was slippery. He crawled on his hands and knees, pushing the light snow ahead of him, so that it slid sideways and dropped off the plane. He crawled carefully up the sloping plane toward the tail and finished clearing off the fusilage. Then he slid back down and cleared each wing. When he had finished the whole job, he stood upright on the top of the plane. His feet began to slip, so he held onto a fir branch to steady himself.

His eyes moved down the lake, on and on into the white distance, then across to the wooded hills on each side. "Doesn't matter where I look," he whispered to himself, "there isn't anyone anywhere except us." How could the world be so empty of people? There wasn't a thing moving anywhere, not even a bird; there wasn't a sound. He dropped to his knees and slid

to the ground. Then he went back to the doorway and climbed inside the plane again. There was the axe he had brought with him. He must not forget to take that back to the cabin.

As he bent to pick it up, he saw the radio dials on the instrument panel. The radio! Perhaps—perhaps it wasn't broken. He let go of the axe and slid down the floor to the instrument panel, reaching for the dials.

The radio came alive with a roar: "And that is the reason why it is Sudbury. . . . Buy Sudbury . . . to feel safe."

David tuned it down. There was a quiet hum, then another voice: "And now five minutes of the latest news. There is still no word on the disappearance of the small private plane in the Sierras yesterday. It is known that the plane carried Jack Milton of Denver, owner of the plane, and his niece and nephew, children of Mr. and Mrs. Thomas Hamilton of Oakland. The plane was on flight from the Oakland airport and should have arrived at Denver about five yesterday evening. Three Army reconnaissance planes took off from McClelland Field this morning. Others have joined the search. The new snow will have covered the plane if it was forced down for any reason. Stay tuned to this station for further news, every hour on the hour—and now—"

David turned it off. It was a good thing his uncle had realized that the snow had to be brushed from the plane, he told himself, but there was something about brushing off the snow that worried him. It worried the back of his mind like a terrier worrying a rat. If it would only come clear! The feeling had been strongest when he stood up on top of the plane, the feeling that something was wrong. He sat back on his heels by the instrument panel and tried to think, but it wouldn't come. Then he realized he was cold.

"Time I was getting back to the cabin," he said to himself. He picked up the axe and was just about to climb out through the doorway when he stopped and looked back at the instrument panel. "Say! I wonder if I could take the radio to the cabin," he said. He slid down to the instrument panel again.

Excitement made his hands all thumbs, and he shook off his mittens. Yes, it was bolted into position—just two bolts, and the wires ran from the radio to—Yes, the battery would be in the baggage compartment behind the back seat. It was just like a car radio.

He scrambled up the sloping floor again for tools—a screw driver and a pair of pliers. That would do it.

He heaved at the pliers and felt the nut give under his hands. And he was sure now that the battery was in the baggage compartment. He would get to it next.

David started toward the cabin with the battery and the radio on a curved piece of aluminum he had hacked from the tail of the plane. It made a wonderful sled, moving along much easier than the one he had made the day before with skis. As he pulled the sled across the lake, he smiled, thinking of what Uncle Jack and Jeannie would say when they saw the radio. He could hear his uncle saying, "Well, what do you know! All the comforts of home!"

Jeannie would clap her hands in the way she had and say, "David!" His thoughts made the time pass quickly, and he was surprised when he realized that he was quite close to the cabin.

The door flew open and Jeannie was there, jumping up and down. David thought she had seen the radio. "Hi!" he yelled at her, waving his arm. "Hi!" But something was wrong. Jeannie did not wave back to him. She was very much excited and she did not look happy; she looked worried. He stopped and called out to her, "What's the matter?" Then he heard the noise. He heard it just as Jeannie shouted at him and pointed into the sky.

"David!" she shouted. "The plane!"

He turned, his eyes going to the sky. The plane was high and far away, moving across the sky, gleaming in the sunlight—but it *was* a plane.

David dropped the sleigh rope and jumped up and down in the snow on his skis. "This way!" he shouted. "Over here! Over here! Here we are!" Then he realized that he was shouting foolishly, that no one in the plane could possibly hear him or see him either, for that matter. He stopped and looked at Jeannie. She stood in the doorway, the tears running down her cheeks as she watched the plane becoming smaller and smaller in the lonely sky.

"It didn't see us, David," she said. "It's gone."

David tried to answer, but there was a lump in his throat that he could not swallow. Then he thought of the radio and pulled the sled to the doorway so that Jeannie could see. "The plane will probably come back." He tried to comfort her. "They fly away; then they circle and come back. That's the way they search for people." He reached the door and patted her shoulder. "It's going to be all right. Look!" He pointed to the sled. "I brought the radio."

"David!" Jeannie was almost as pleased as he had thought she would be. "It must have been hard to get it out," she said, "but it will be so nice for Uncle Jack." Together they pulled the sled up and through the doorway.

When David had told about hearing the news on the radio, they set to work to connect it. Uncle Jack did not seem worried about the plane flying off. "We know they are hunting for us now," he explained, "because David heard it on the radio. And they are bound to see the wreck of our plane when they fly over this lake."

He seemed much pleased to have the radio. "What do you know?" he said. "A mechanic in the family!" He checked it over to see that it was connected correctly. "Good for you, David. How did you know enough about it to get it out?"

David felt happy and warm with pleasure, but he felt awkward too. His father usually just patted his shoulder when he did something well. Uncle Jack talked a lot about it.

"I—I guess I just followed the wires," David said. "I knew they had to go to a battery if it worked like a car radio."

"But how did you lift the heavy battery?" Uncle Jack asked.

"I used a piece of rope, here—like this," David explained. He got the piece of rope and made a loop in it. "I got the wires off it and got it loose from its frame. Then I made a rope sling for it like this, and lowered it down from the baggage compartment."

"Well!" Uncle Jack was looking at him again. "That was a very smart thing to do. I—"

There was no mistaking the sound. It was the plane again, or another one, and this time much closer. David and Jeannie burst out of the door to see.

The plane was high, but it flew right down the lake, going fast, its great wings flashing in the sunlight. In a moment it was gone. David and Jeannie looked at each other. Then Jeannie turned to the cabin door. "It didn't stop or do anything, Uncle Jack," she said in a small voice.

David felt a great weight on his heart. The plane hadn't shown any sign at all. But Uncle Jack was smiling. "A plane can't stop that easily," he explained. "What happens is that the pilot sees something, then flies on and turns in a big sweeping circle and comes in lower next time to take a good look. In a minute you'll hear him fly down the lake again. Then he'll radio back to Oakland or wherever he comes from, to tell them he has found our plane. Put your jackets on and run out, away from the cabin, so that he can see that we're all right. Hurry!"

They pulled on their jackets as they rushed for the door. Then they were out in the snow, waiting, watching. The sun was lower in the sky now. It was afternoon, David realized, long past his usual lunch time. It must have taken him a long time to get the radio out of the plane. The shadows lay to the east of the trees and the cabin—long blue shadows.

There was no sound as David and Jeannie waited. Jeannie swung her arms around and shifted her weight, first to one foot, then to the other. The minutes ticked by. She stopped moving and looked up at David. He knew there would be a question in her eyes, and he did not look at her because he did not know what to say. He scraped a little spot in the snow with his boot, and kept his eyes on that spot. Then he carefully scraped the snow back into the little spot. The minutes went by.

"They aren't coming back, are they, David." Jeannie's voice was almost a whisper, it was so low. It wasn't a question. She knew. He felt her hand in his, and they moved together up the steps and into the cabin.

Uncle Jack sat on the bed. He looked ill; his face was white and strained. He did not say anything for some time; then he asked, "Did you get all the snow off the top of the plane, David?"

"Yes," David told him, "every bit. I remember when I stood up to look down the lake, from the top of the plane. There was just one little bit of snow on the plane, and I got down and brushed it off."

Uncle Jack turned to look into the fire. "Guess we should build it up, David," he said. "It's getting cold in here."

David couldn't move. In his mind he was seeing down the lake again as he had seen it that morning, standing on the newly-swept plane. Now he knew what had worried him after he had cleaned off the plane. When he stood up on top of it, he had been holding onto something—a fir branch. *Their plane was under the trees!* That was why there was such a little snow on it. That was why the searching plane had not come back. Their wrecked plane was under the trees and couldn't be seen from the air. David turned toward the bed. "Uncle Jack," he said, "I know—"

"You know what, David?"

David, seeing how ill his uncle looked, knew he must have been in such pain yesterday that he didn't realize his plane was under the trees. Also, he knew that Uncle Jack could not do anything about it now, because he had a broken leg. David realized that he must keep this great worry to himself. Somehow he must do something.

"You know what, David?"

"I know the fire needs some wood," David said. He added some small pieces and two big logs.

"Isn't anyone going to come and rescue us, David?" Jeannie asked.

"Yes, they'll come, Jeannie. Don't you worry," David said. "It's going to take a little longer than we thought, but they'll come." He hoped he looked braver than he felt. "It won't be today I guess." He managed to smile at her as he said it.

Their uncle was smiling, too. "You can do other things besides bring radios, I see," Uncle Jack said.

David was not quite sure what Uncle Jack meant, but he knew that they weren't talking about radios at all. He turned back to Jeannie. "I'm hungry," he said. "Aren't you?"

Jeannie nodded her head. "Yes, I am, too, but what are we going to eat?"

"Beans," David told her as he went to build up the fire in the cookstove, "and more beans and more beans and more beans—because I'm just about the hungriest boy that ever lived."

But he knew that the big cold empty place inside him wasn't going to be helped by beans. It was cold and empty and sick because he was afraid—and he could not show Jeannie or Uncle Jack that he was afraid. Somehow he had to work it out by himself. He had never felt so alone before in his life. Did being grown-up mean feeling this way sometimes?

CHAPTER FIVE

Exploring Silver Lake

DAVID came out of miles and miles of sleep to realize that his uncle was calling him and Jeannie too. Another morning had come, and David sat up in bed in the bright sunlight streaming through the window, and looked across at Uncle Jack.

"Thought you were never going to come alive this morning." Uncle Jack smiled at him.

"Uncle Jack!" Jeannie's head came out from under her blankets. "Why are you making so much noise?" She stretched and yawned. "What day is it?"

"Let me see now—" Uncle Jack frowned. "So much has happened that I have to stop and think. We took off from the Oakland airport on the twenty-seventh of December. That was yesterday—no, the day before yesterday. Yesterday was the twenty-eighth and today is the twenty-ninth of December."

"It will soon be New Year's Eve," Jeannie said.

Uncle Jack grinned at them, sitting up in their beds with their blankets held close around them. "Did you hear the owls last night?" he asked.

It all came back to David like a wave of cold, icy water washing over him. Yesterday one rescue plane had come, but no one could know they were here because Uncle Jack's plane was hidden by the trees. It couldn't be seen from the air. "Uncle Jack doesn't know," David thought, "and I can't tell him because he has a broken leg and can't do anything."

Yes, he heard the owls as he lay in the dark trying to think of a plan to save Jeannie and Uncle Jack. The deep, lonely, hollow sounds of the owls had come to him through the walls of the cabin, underlining the fact that he was lost with Jeannie and Uncle Jack in the mountains, and that no one knew even where to look for them. And he had realized that growing up was sometimes like this, trying to think for yourself and for others too. Yes, he had heard the owls, but he could not tell Jeannie and Uncle Jack.

"How long—" David paused to word his question

carefully— "how long before you could get around on a crutch with that leg?" Then he held tight to the blanket, waiting for the answer.

"I don't know, David." Uncle Jack's voice was harsh, his eyes worried. "It isn't set, you see. It might become much worse if I tried to get around. I'm going to have to stay right here in this bed until someone comes for us, I guess." He stopped, looking from David to Jeannie. "Why did you ask, David?"

"Guess I'll light the fire," David said. He avoided his uncle's eyes by jumping out of bed and tugging hard at his flying boots. "These boots," he said, "they're cold."

Breakfast was pancakes again. David thought they did not taste quite so good as they had the morning before, but Uncle Jack told Jeannie they were better than ever, and Jeannie laughed and blushed. She was pretty when she blushed, David thought. She looked like Mother.

Uncle Jack talked fast and ate fast, as if he had to hurry to get on with something. As soon as he had finished his pancakes and ham and coffee, he said, "Now, I have an idea. It isn't a very good idea because you two have to do all the work, but I think you can do it. Come over here and I'll show you. Bring that piece of pencil on the table with you."

When Jeannie and David were beside him, he leaned over and began to draw on the floor with the pencil. "I am drawing a map of Silver Lake," he told them. He outlined the lake, marking the location of their plane and the cabin. Then he moved the pencil along the line of the lake from their cabin.

"If you go on your skis, along the ice toward the head of the lake, you will pass other cabins. They may have someone living in them, or there may be supplies in them that we can use. Or there may be a road near enough to the lake so that if you listen carefully you can hear cars passing along it. I think they keep some of the roads around here open in winter, and I know that Route 88 goes just north of the lake. If it is open, you may hear cars going along it. Don't try to reach it, David. Just listen for cars."

David had a question. "Don't you think Jeannie should stay with you?" he suggested. It would be much nicer to have Jeannie with him, but who would look after Uncle Jack?

"I'll be fine here," Uncle Jack answered. "I'm going to have you two push my bed near enough to the

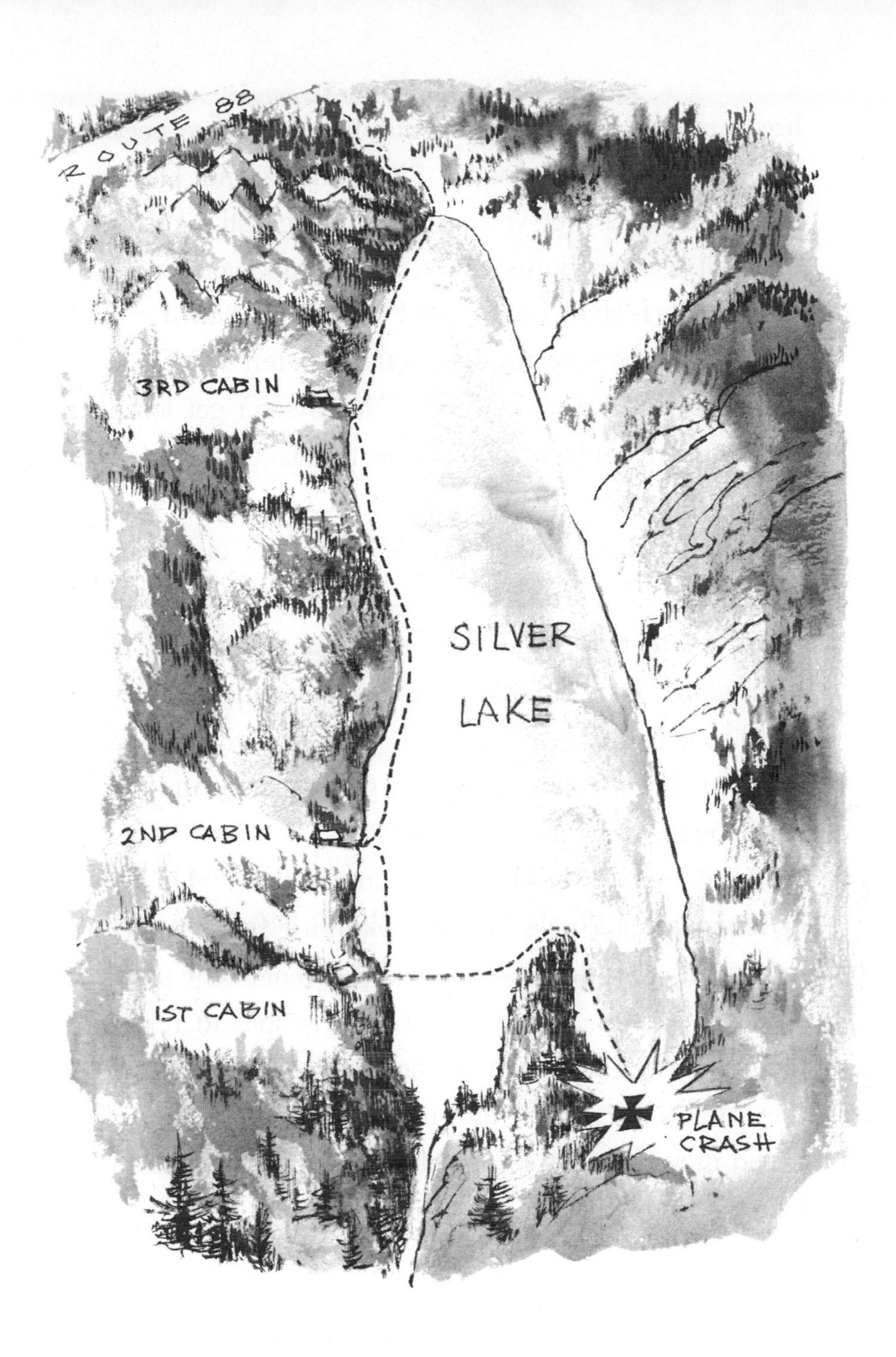
ROUTE 88
3RD CABIN
SILVER
LAKE
2ND CABIN
1ST CABIN
PLANE
CRASH

fire so that I can add some wood when the fire needs it." He thought a moment. "You understand, David, that I would not let you and Jeannie go off like this unless it was really necessary, and I hope you understand that I shall be worried about you until you return. So be sure to do exactly as I tell you."

Uncle Jack wasn't smiling. "You won't get lost if you both remember to stay on the lake, but right close to the shore all the way. Never go so far from the shore that you lose sight of the lake, and come back along the tracks that your skis make going out. Don't try to take short cuts; stick to the tracks you make going out." He thought a moment more. "And don't be gone too long," he said. "I think you can get to the end of the lake, but don't go farther. And if it gets cloudy, turn back at once."

David studied the little map on the floor. He felt better now that Uncle Jack was planning for them. It helped him to forget his unsolved problem of the plane under the trees. They might find people to rescue them; they might find more food. They might—yes, they might meet a deer or a moose or a bear. A *bear!* David moved to the corner of the cabin. "Guess I'll take the rifle," he said.

He busied himself with the rifle, stroking its gleaming stock, turning it over in his hands. He did not look at his uncle, but he told himself that Uncle Jack shouldn't object. He had to protect Jeannie, didn't he? He did not know how to load and fire the rifle, but he thought it best to wait a minute before asking Uncle Jack for the information.

"What are you planning to kill, David?" Uncle Jack spoke quietly.

David looked up quickly, his eyes meeting his uncle's. The question had caught him off guard. "Why, nothing," he said.

Uncle Jack's eyes were hard. "Men carry rifles for just one thing, David. Only if they plan to kill something."

"Well—" David looked down at the rifle, his eyes on the barrel. Then he sighted along the barrel, pointing the rifle toward the window. "The ham is just about gone," he said. He found it hard to put his thoughts into words. "I might see a deer."

"And do you know how to skin out a deer?"

David felt angry. He had been put into a position that was hard to defend. "No, but I could do it, I guess, if you told me how."

"People who carry guns are often in far more danger than if they were without them," Uncle Jack said. "You and Jeannie will be safer without it."

David sighed and put the rifle in the corner, patting its gleaming stock one last time. He reached for his jacket and picked up the axe.

"Just a minute!" Jeannie was wrapping a package. "I'm taking some cold pancakes for when we get hungry," she told him.

Uncle Jack sat quiet on the bed, a frown on his face. "You do understand, don't you, David?" he asked.

"Yes, sure." David did not meet his uncle's eyes. He wanted to forget the whole thing now.

"A great deal depends on you," Uncle Jack said as David opened the door.

"Oh! It's cold!" Jeannie shouted. "Let's race, David. It will get us warm."

David's mind was busy with his uncle's last words. And the worry of the plane—too far under the trees to be seen—was like a toothache, so that he needed to do something to drive it out of his mind. "Guess we shouldn't race," he said. "It'll tire us out sooner, but"—he laughed back at Jeannie—"beat you to that big rock on the shore over there!" He was off as he said it.

"You wait!" Jeannie shouted. "That's not fair. You started without saying, 'One, two, three, go.' " She raced after him as fast as she could. Their skis hissed over the snow in the quiet sunlit air.

David reached the rock first and stood listening to the quiet. Suddenly he noticed tracks in the snow, tracks that came down to the shore of the lake and then moved along in the direction they would take. He bent over to study them.

Jeannie followed, bending to stare at the tracks in her turn. "What made them?" she asked.

David could see, in his mind, a book on a shelf in the school library—a book that told about animals and showed pictures of their tracks and how to identify them in the snow. He could even see some of the tracks as they appeared in the book, but he couldn't remember what made the tracks. If he had been able to read what was printed under the pictures in the book— Why were there so many times when you just *had* to know how to read?

"It had sharp feet," he told Jeannie, "because—see —they sank into the snow. But I don't think it was

very heavy, because they didn't sink down very far. There are bunches of tracks—see, over there." He pointed to the next group of tracks. "It was either a very long animal, or it was jumping." He pointed to the next group of tracks.

"Look at those," he said. "There's a book in our

library at school that has tracks in it like this. I don't know any more except that the book was written by Ernest Thompson Seton. I remember that because Joe told me he'd never heard of the name Seton."

"David!" Jeannie's eyes were shining. "You're reading the tracks just the way our teacher says the Indians do. You can tell all sorts of things about the animals from the tracks."

David felt a sudden flood of pleasure warm him. Maybe it was a kind of reading, he thought, and he could do this kind, but he did not know enough even here. He wanted to know what kind of animal it was. A cold chill ran down his back. Then Jeannie voiced his unspoken fears. "Do you think it would kill us if it found us, David?"

"No, silly." He felt cross with Jeannie for saying it. "Uncle Jack says there's nothing to be afraid of up here." He moved on suddenly, following the tracks along the lake, gripping the axe tight in his right hand just below the head.

The tracks went along the lake ahead of them, right past the next cabin, and David would have liked to go on, too, for the cabin looked more lonely and uninviting than theirs had looked when he first found it. He turned aside and made for the cabin, his hand tighter on the axe. "Maybe we can find some more food in here," he said.

He pried the door open with his axe. There was no lock on this door; it was just nailed shut. As it creaked open, David moved cautiously into the doorway. They had left the skis, at the foot of the steps, turned around ready for them to start again.

The cabin was much like theirs, consisting of one huge room and a fireplace, but it was not so well finished. They spoke in whispers as they moved into the dark, cold room. They stood in the middle of it, holding hands until their eyes became used to the dark. Then they went across to the kitchen part and opened the cupboard doors.

The cupboards were bare except for a few empty jars and bottles. There was nothing of any use to them. "Let's go," Jeannie said, moving toward the door. David followed her at once, glad to be out in the sunshine again. He hammered the nails of the door back into place with the head of the axe. They put their skis on and glided out onto the surface of the lake, heading toward the third cabin in the distance.

This cabin was set back farther from the lake than the other two and was larger. It had a wing built onto one end. A landing pier reached well out into the lake. David and Jeannie skied to the pier, slipped off their skis, and waded up to the door. This cabin had a lock, and David pried it off with the axe. As the door creaked inward, there was a rush of cold air.

When David and Jeannie peered inside, they saw that a window in the opposite wall was open. A drift of snow lay across the floor almost to the doorway where they stood. Because the window was out, this cabin was lighter than the last one. David stepped inside and Jeannie followed. Then they heard a strange clicking sound—click, click, click—click, click, click.

David stiffened and felt Jeannie's hand tighten on his arm. There was an instant's quiet; then Jeannie turned quickly to the door. "Let's get out of here, David."

She was part way down the pier in seconds. David needed only her running to start him; in a moment he was beside her. Jeannie's eyes were huge as she looked at him. "What *was* it?"

"I don't know." There was a sinking feeling in his

stomach. He gripped the axe and moved a step back toward the door.

"David, don't!" Jeannie was beside him in a minute. "David, you can't."

It would have been nice to let himself be persuaded, but David knew he had to find out what was in there. They couldn't go back and tell Uncle Jack they had heard a strange noise, so they had not looked into the last cabin. "Maybe it's just something that got loose, a board or something," David said, trying to convince himself. "Yes, it's just a loose board or something—I hope." He moved cautiously back to the open door and peered in, holding his breath.

The queer clicking noise came again—click, click, click. Then there was a small grunting noise, and David saw a dark shape move out from behind the kitchen stove.

"Look out!" He found himself running down the pier to Jeannie and yelling as he ran, "It's coming!"

"Oh, David!" Jeannie clutched his arm and stared at the cabin. They listened, not knowing whether to flee or stay. Then the dark shape appeared in the doorway, along with the clicking and grunting noise, and the animal came out into the sunlight.

"A porcupine!" David let all the air out of his lungs with a rush. Then he was laughing and jumping up and down as he shouted, "A porcupine, a porcupine!"

"Will it hurt us?" Jeannie was still fearful.

"They don't hurt anyone who doesn't hurt them." David was happy that he knew.

They watched the porcupine as it moved away into the forest, its quills rising and falling, making the queer clicking noise. It was grunting and grumbling to itself like a small pig.

"The Indians call them quill pigs," David told Jeannie.

They watched it disappear into the forest; then they returned to the cabin and went inside, still laughing with relief.

They discovered where the porcupine had gnawed its way through the edge of a cupboard and had eaten something there—something that it liked so well that it had even chewed and eaten the wood to get the last taste. Then they turned to examine the contents of another cupboard, which had not been disturbed.

"More beans!" Jeannie put her hands into the depths of the cupboard and pulled out the cans. "Ugh," she said, "I'm tired of beans."

"Tea," David said.

"Chocolate bars!" Jeannie's voice thrilled as she discovered them.

"Don't eat them," David warned her sharply. "We don't know if some of this stuff is bad."

"More cans." Jeannie pulled them out, reading the labels as she did so. "This one's canned ham, David. This is salmon, and this one is sausage. Mmmm, that sounds good."

David counted, his gloved finger touching the cans. "Nine of them," he said. His eyes swept the empty cupboards. "I guess that's all." It made him very hungry. There would not be any more food after this. There weren't any more cabins, and the food in their own cabin was almost gone. He turned to see Jeannie unwrapping the package she had brought with her.

"One's for you," she said, holding the package toward him.

"Pancakes!" David realized how hungry he was. He reached for one; then his hand stopped. "Did you leave any for Uncle Jack?"

"No." Jeannie folded her cold pancake and bit into it. "He said he almost never eats lunch."

David turned his pancake over in his hand and thought of Uncle Jack. When he could wait no longer, he took a huge bite. Never had anything tasted so good.

He gathered the cans into a pile. "There must be something we can wrap these in," he said.

"Here!" Jeannie held out the sacking that the porcupine had torn from the window. "We can wrap them in this," she said.

David tied the ends to make a sort of bag. They left the cabin, carrying the cans, and skied down the pier.

It was early afternoon when they reached the end of the lake. Their eyes followed the back sweep of the shore line where it curved down the eastern side. There were no other cabins that they could see, no smoke, no people, nothing. They listened, but there was no sound.

"I'm going to climb up the hill here," David said, putting down the bag of heavy cans. "Uncle Jack would want me to take one look, to see if there are other cabins or a road, and I want to listen. Uncle Jack said we might hear cars on Route 88 if it's open. You stay here," he told her, "right here so that I can see you all the time and you can see me."

He left her there on the shore of the lake, because he realized that she wasn't as strong as he was. Even he was getting tired, and they still had to go all the way back to the cabin.

"There just has to be a traveled road over this hill—a road, or a house with smoke coming from the chimney, or something," David told himself. Up he climbed, up and up, through the scattered pines. It was slow going among the trees on skis. He stopped often in the clear places so that he could look down and see Jeannie. He reached the top at last, certain that there would be something for them over the hill.

But there was nothing to be seen from the top but the cold and lonely hills. Some were pine covered; some were bare of trees, with just rocks and snow. Nothing moved across them. If there was a road, no one had used it lately; there were no tracks in the snow. David turned and moved down the hill again. He must think. A picture of his father and mother came to him, and he felt the hot tears in his eyes. He shook them away angrily. Jeannie would be very tired; he must get her back to the cabin, back to Uncle Jack. And he could not see the sun now; it was getting cloudy. They must hurry.

They moved off, over the tracks they had made, saying nothing. There was nothing to say. Uncle Jack had been right; their tracks were easy to follow. They would not get lost if they got back to their cabin before it snowed. David glided along, absorbed in his thoughts; then he heard Jeannie crying.

"What's the matter, Jeannie?" He skied close to her and put his arm around her shoulders as he spoke.

"I guess I'm so tired," Jeannie sobbed, "and I want to go home to Mother and Dad."

David felt a lump gather in his own throat. He was tired, too. The cans he carried seemed to grow heavier and heavier. In his mind's eye he could see his father at the office, his mother at home. She would have the radio playing as she finished the lunch dishes, and Patty would be curled up asleep on the kitchen floor, in Mother's way as she moved from sink to cupboards.

David swallowed the lump in his throat. "We'll soon be at the cabin," he said, "and Uncle Jack will be feeling bad because of his leg, so we must cheer him up."

David thought at first that it was Jeannie's mention of home that made the day seem so dark; then he realized that the sun had disappeared behind the clouds. There was a film over the whole sky. The wind was beginning to rise, curling the snow in little whirls ahead of them as they moved along with the wind at their backs.

As they went slowly along the lake shore, the sky grew gradually darker, the cloud-bank seemed to deepen, and the wind began to whistle through the pines. Ahead of them a tiny drift of snow busily filled in the windward side of their tracks.

Suddenly David heard a noise above the rushing sound of the wind, and he glanced at Jeannie. She did not give any sign that she had heard it, but David knew it was the noise of a plane. It was traveling high and fast, far above the low clouds. Even if it were under the clouds, the people up there could not see the wrecked plane under the trees. What was he going to do? He must think of something.

"He has a good fire on, anyway," shouted Jeannie.

David had been so busy with his thoughts that he had not seen the home cabin when it came in sight. Jeannie was right; there was a curl of blue smoke coming from the chimney. That was some comfort, he thought; they were warm and had a warm place to stay. There was lots of wood, but the food was running short. David thought of the few cans in the bag he carried.

"Hi!" Uncle Jack smiled at them from his bed close to the fireplace as they came in, stamping the snow from their feet. "Did you have fun?"

"Oh!" Jeannie dropped into a chair. "I'm tired," she gasped.

David watched his uncle. His face was smiling, but his eyes, searching the bag that lay open on the floor, held a question that David knew he wanted to ask.

"We saw a porcupine!" Jeannie said.

"A porcupine!" Uncle Jack's eyes lit up at that. "A porcupine," he repeated.

Now why should Uncle Jack be so pleased that they had seen a porcupine? David wondered. Adults were strange people. "No people and no road," he told Uncle Jack.

"No?" his uncle answered, but David saw that his thoughts were elsewhere. "A porcupine!" he said. Then he reached toward the radio and turned the knobs. "Almost forgot. Four o'clock news." There was an electric stillness in the cabin as the three listened.

"Still no news of the missing small plane. . . . Ground parties will be sent out as soon as the plane is located. . . ." David held his breath waiting to hear. "Planes have flown shuttle service. . . . And with the coming storm, visibility will. . . ."

The news ended, and Uncle Jack snapped off the radio. "Well," he said. "Well—"

"I'll get wood," David said. He reached for his flying boots.

"Then we'll have dinner." Uncle Jack's bright voice reached him as he went out of the door into the dark gray world. It was snowing now, and the snow on the ground was as white as the whitest paper, and smooth except where his feet sank into it. He made an *X* with the axe blade in the new snow, then another one, and way back in his mind he heard his teacher say, "Twenty." His mind was half busy with the threat of the storm and half with the two X's in the snow. "That's twenty in Roman numerals," he thought. The new snow was a fine place for writing.

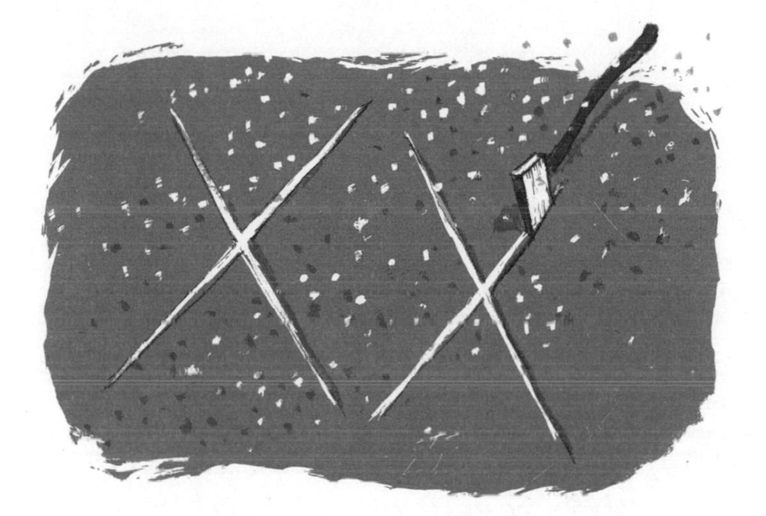

CHAPTER SIX

The Storm

DAVID finished splitting some wood and carried it inside. The fire snapped brightly and made dancing shadows on the walls. Uncle Jack was propped up against his pillows, giving directions to Jeannie.

"We're making baking-powder biscuits, David," Jeannie called to him, waving a floury hand. "Uncle Jack is telling me how to do it." She turned to the big mixing bowl again.

David shook his head to clear his mind of the darkness and the snow. Uncle Jack was doing his best to keep things cheerful for them, and Jeannie was, too; so David realized that he must help. "Good!" he said. "I'm hungry." He sat down in front of the fireplace, putting his cold hands between his face and the hot fire.

All through the time they ate supper and washed dishes, the storm hammered at the cabin. Wind blew down the chimney, sometimes scattering ashes out on the stone hearth.

At ten o'clock Uncle Jack turned on the radio. There was quiet in the cabin except for the swish of the wind, the crackle of the fire, and the whisper of the snow against the dark window. Then the voice came into the room.

"Good evening. This is Logan Bates. Here is the news. This evening saw the passing of a landmark. The fine old . . ."

Dimly David realized that he spoke of a building he knew, a building in San Francisco, but he waited for word of himself and of Uncle Jack and Jeannie. Finally it came.

"Still no news of the three people who disappeared in a small private plane on December twenty-seventh. Flying conditions in the area have been poor; however, there is no thought of abandoning the search. . . ."

Uncle Jack snapped off the radio, and then there was only the sound of the wind outside, and three people inside who were tired, discouraged, and lonely.

"Well!" Uncle Jack was the first to break the

silence. "I guess we'd better get to bed. It's sure to clear in the morning, and then we'll have to get busy." He looked at Jeannie, but she said nothing. His eyes turned to David.

David nodded his head. He did not feel that he could speak right then. He got up slowly and took off his boots.

The fire had died down to a dull red glow, but the wind had risen higher and howled around the cabin like a wolf. David could hear Uncle Jack breathing deeply as he lay on his bed, his broken leg stretched out stiffly under the blanket. David could still see, in the flickering shadows, Jeannie's blankets moving up and down slowly as she breathed gently.

Uncle Jack and Jeannie were asleep; he must go to sleep, too. There wasn't any use lying awake, thinking of the plane under the trees and of the food supply getting less and less. And yet he *must* think of something to do. He could not let Jeannie and Uncle Jack starve here and never be found. He couldn't move the plane, of course. Could he possibly climb the trees and chop off enough branches so that it would show? There *must* be something he could do. He thought back to the porcupine. Why had Uncle Jack been so interested when they had told him about the porcupine? Perhaps it was good to eat! It would be easy to catch, and he could probably kill it with the axe if he did not get so close as to be hit by its swinging spiny tail. The thought of killing it made him feel a little sick, but he might have to.

David never knew quite when it happened. Afterward he wondered if he had dreamed it. He had been thinking about the plane and the snow, and his mind had wandered back over the day, to seeing the animal tracks in the snow, to Jeannie's surprise that he could read the tracks, to splitting wood while the snow fell in white flakes, to writing the XX in the snow with the axe blade, and how clean and clear the two letters were. Things got jumbled together somehow, and he was just about asleep when it all came clear.

He sat up in bed and was suddenly wide awake. That was it! That was the answer—*snow writing!* He could do it. He was not aware that the blankets had fallen off until he shivered in the rapidly cooling cabin.

He could! He could do it. The animal this morning had made tracks in the snow that anyone could read who knew about wild life. And he, David, could make tracks in the snow with the axe. He had done so this evening, and anyone could read what he wrote in the snow. . . . Suppose he wrote big letters on the snow-covered lake. Someone in an airplane could read the letters. They would not have to see the wrecked plane. He could call rescuers by *tramping out words in BIG LETTERS* on the lake.

This was such a big thought that he sat there in the cold for a long time; then he lay down. He must not forget it. In the morning Uncle Jack would want him to go and sweep the snow off the plane again. He would tell Jeannie, and they would write a message in the snow on the lake, a great big one with letters ten or twenty feet high.

David did not know how long he lay there, no longer hearing the storm outside, thoughts racing through his head. It would work; it had to work. It was no good with snow falling and wind blowing, but perhaps in the morning the snow would have stopped and the sky would be clear and then . . . and . . . then . . .

David overslept the next morning. He came out of deep miles of sleep to hear Jeannie calling, "David," then again, "David, wake up!"

He came awake, sitting up in bed. "What's wrong?"

"It's time to get up, David." Jeannie was peering at him from her nest of blankets. "Uncle Jack and I are hungry. We want you to get up and light the fire so I can get breakfast."

"Oh!" David lay back, gathering the threads of yesterday together. "What time is it?"

"Eight." Uncle Jack had his arm out of bed, looking at his wrist watch.

"And what day?" David yawned.

"December thirtieth," Jeannie said.

David got out of bed, shivering and reaching for his boots. "It's cold," he said.

Jeannie laughed. "I'm glad I'm a girl," she said. "Girls never have to get up first and light the fires."

"Mother does," David reminded her sharply.

"Pooh!" Jeannie made a face at him from her blanket. "Mother just has to turn a button on the automatic furnace."

"The wonders of civilization," Uncle Jack said.

David did not know what Uncle Jack meant. He ran to the fireplace and began to whittle shavings. Poor Jeannie, he thought, and Uncle Jack looking so old and worried. They did not know what he knew. David hugged himself as he finished the shavings. He knew now how to save all of them—if it had stopped snowing.

"Is it snowing?" he asked suddenly. It was very important that it stop snowing. He went to the door.

"David!" Jeannie looked cross. "Light the fire first."

David opened the door. There was a rush of cold air, and a soft drift against the door collapsed into the room. The air was a dark gray, filled with snow—snow—snow. It seemed to be everywhere. It lay thick on the ground, piled high against anything that David could see in the gray light, swirling and falling, so that the world was a whirling world of snow. Beyond were the swaying pines, moaning in the wind, and beyond them the gray swirling nothingness of the snow where the lake began. David closed the door.

"Is it, David?" Uncle Jack sat up, not seeming to feel the cold. The careworn look was deep in his eyes.

"Yes," David told him. Yes, it was snowing and his plan would have to wait, because the snow would cover any tracks he made. Planes could not fly in this weather, anyway.

Uncle Jack lay back on his bed. David returned to the fireplace and reached for the matches. He felt warm inside in spite of the gray day, because now he knew what to do. He struck a match, and there was a sudden flash of light in the dark cabin. The shavings caught, and the light danced across the dark walls.

"At last," Jeannie sighed. "I think I'm frozen to death."

"What's for breakfast?" David asked her.

"Biscuits and sausage, I guess." Jeannie came out from under her blanket.

"We'll have to go a bit easy on the food." Uncle Jack's voice had a harsh sound. "I want you to bring all of it here to me, David," he said, "so I can see what is left. We'll have to go a bit easy until the snow stops and you can go to sweep off the plane again. We can't be rescued, you know, if the planes looking for us can't see our plane."

That was the longest day of David's life. They had breakfast, a small breakfast, rationed, as Uncle Jack directed. David felt hungrier after breakfast than he had before. He helped Jeannie sweep the cabin. He whittled enough shavings to start the fires for a whole week. He walked up and down the cabin, up and down. Nine o'clock passed, then ten; the hours dragged. Every little while he went to the door, and still it snowed; still the air was filled with the whirling whiteness that blotted out the lake and everything else. Lunch time came, one o'clock; they had a little bit to eat, a few beans warmed up.

"I hate beans," Jeannie said. "After we're rescued I'm not going to eat another bean in my life, not for ever and ever and ever."

David laughed. He could not help it. He had lost his taste for beans, too, but she did look so funny sitting there pushing a bean around and around on her plate.

David noticed that Uncle Jack did not laugh. He had eaten every one of his beans, and he had kept the smallest share for himself, too. He had said again that he was not hungry, but David knew that Uncle Jack had another reason for not eating much. And knowing what that reason was, David could not eat much himself.

It was three o'clock when the snow finally stopped. David had gone to the door so many times that for a moment he did not realize, when he looked out into the white world, that the wind had gone down and that the snow had stopped falling. He turned to close the door; then he swung it wide. "It's stopped," he whispered. It was so white and still outside that it seemed wrong to speak aloud.

"I think it's too late to go out to sweep off the plane now, David," Uncle Jack said. "It's three, and it will be dark soon."

"No!" David sprung into action at once. He ran for his jacket. "We can make it," he said. "Come on, Jeannie."

"It's too far, David," Uncle Jack warned. "You mustn't go!"

"I'm not going to the plane." David was struggling

into his jacket. "I have to get wood and—other things." He looked at Jeannie, slowly putting on her coat. "Come on, Jeannie!" he shouted.

He pulled her through the door while she was still putting her mittens on, and slammed it shut.

"David!" Jeannie never liked to be made to hurry. "We can get our mittens on first, I should hope," she said.

"Jeannie! Look," he said. He took one of the skis that leaned against the cabin and, using the point of it, printed in the snow D-A-V-I-D.

Jeannie looked at the letters, then at David. "You didn't bring me out just to see you write your name in the silly old snow, did you?" she asked.

"Can't you see?" David was jumping around on the steps in his excitement. "We'll write in the snow for when the planes come."

Jeannie could not understand. A frown appeared between her eyes. "Why?"

"Because—" Then David realized that he must go back to the beginning. "Our plane is under the trees," he said. "No plane in the sky could see our plane even if it is swept clear of snow, because it's too far under the trees. It went in there as it crashed. I know because I stood up on the wing of our plane and I could touch the big fir branches above the wing."

Jeannie was beginning to understand. "Do you mean they never could see our plane, David?" she asked.

"That's right. That's why the one we saw day before yesterday flew right on. There wasn't anything for them to see. So we have to write a message for the planes when they come to look for us."

"Oh," Jeannie cried. She stood on the steps, her chin pulled down into her collar, shivering in the still cold. "Will anyone ever find us? Does Uncle Jack know about this?"

"No, he does not." David picked up the skis and set them on the snow ready for Jeannie and him to shove off. "I can't tell him. He couldn't do anything about it anyway."

Jeannie fitted her feet into the ski bindings. "What are we going to do?" she asked.

"What I just showed you." David shoved his feet into the bindings and pushed off from the steps. "We are going to go out on the lake, and then we are going to print the biggest words you ever saw."

"Oh!" David saw her face light up as she realized

what he had been trying to tell her. "I'll help," she assured him, "and I'm sure it will work."

"You'll have to help," David said. "I'm not very good in spelling, remember?"

He never minded admitting to Jeannie that he was not very good at reading and spelling. She always understood.

"What will we say?" Jeannie's eyes were sparkling as she moved over the snow.

David had the words ready. He had thought about them last night and all this morning. "I think we should print the word *help* in big letters in the middle of the lake. Then we'll print *Jack Milton,* because Uncle Jack is our pilot. Then we'll make a big arrow pointing toward the cabin."

Jeannie was quiet as she moved along on her skis. "I think we should add *All Safe,*" she said. "If Daddy is in the plane or if the plane can radio back, they would all want to know if we are safe."

David had to admit she was right. "All right," he said. "We'll print, *Help—Jack Milton—All Safe—* and then make a big arrow." He looked at the sky. "The clouds are low and thick today, but if we get the letters made, a plane may come in the morning."

Jeannie stood at one end while David took off his skis and waded up and down the huge space they had decided upon. It was hard and warm work, but he wanted to make the letters very big and very deep so they could be seen easily from thc air. Jeannie told him how to spell, and after a long time of wading, the words were printed:

JACK MILTON   HELP

ALL SAFE   ⟶

While David got his breath, they admired their work. "I bet it looks good from the air," Jeannie said.

David looked at the sky. "I guess we might as well go back now," he told her. And they turned away from the center of the lake and started to ski for the cabin while David told how the idea had come to him.

"You're smart, David," Jeannie said, looking at him with a proud smile.

And David felt the warm feeling passing over him that always came when Jeannie or his mother or father praised him. "I just hope a plane comes now," he said.

David heard it first, when they were half way to the cabin—the roar of a plane motor! "Where?" He gazed at the sky, trying to spot the plane.

"There—" Jeannie was pointing, her arm high, "There!"

David saw it break through the cloud bank at the far end of the lake. It was flying low, to get under the clouds, and it was traveling very fast. It thundered down the lake, its dark gray shape rushing along above the snow. There was a shattering roar and a flash as it passed. Then it swept up into the clouds again and was gone.

"Oh!" Jeannie said. "It came, David."

"Yes!" Jumping about in excitement, David had lost one ski. He was standing with one foot in a ski binding and the other sunk deep in the snow. "It'll come back now, after it circles," he told her. "Then I guess it'll land on the lake. We have to hurry." He fumbled with the loose ski, his fingers all thumbs as he worked. "There!" He stood up. "Now we'll get to Uncle Jack and tell him—" But he realized something was wrong. His movements slowed, and he glanced across at Jeannie. She did not seem to notice. David skied on beside her again for a short time; then he stopped. Jeannie stopped, too.

"What is it, David?" she asked.

"Listen." David held his breath. He held it as long as he could; then he breathed out and in quickly and held it again. There was the snow and the dark grayness of the day and the stillness. That was all. "They're not coming back," he told her. "They would have been here by now."

After a while they moved on toward the cabin, and David realized that Jeannie was crying, but he could not move over to comfort her because there wasn't anything he could say.

"What's going to happen to us?" Jeannie asked, gliding along on her skis, the tears running down her face.

"I don't know," David said. He didn't like to think about it. "Let's go tell Uncle Jack. He's a man. Perhaps he can think of something." But David knew deep down in his heart that there wasn't anything Uncle Jack could do, nor anything he could do, nor Jeannie.

They reached the cabin, and David leaned the skis against the cabin wall as Jeannie went inside. Then he followed her. As he took a last look outside before closing the door, he saw that the snow flakes were beginning to fall again.

CHAPTER SEVEN

Word from the Outside World

DAVID stood in front of the fireplace. His hands were cold, but he did not hold them out to the flames. One thought chased itself around his brain. It hadn't worked after all. His wonderful idea was no good.

Jeannie was sitting on the floor beside Uncle Jack's bed, her head on the blankets, Uncle Jack's hand stroking her bright hair as she talked.

"The plane is under the trees, so no one can see it," Jeannie said, her voice muffled by tears and the blanket. "But they can't see David's snow sign either. What are we going to do, Uncle Jack?"

Uncle Jack's eyes sought David's. "What does she mean by 'snow sign'?"

"When our plane crashed, it slid under the trees," David told him. "I don't think anyone could see it from the air. I stood up on the wing when I swept the snow off it the first time it snowed, and I found that the branches of the fir trees come right down over it."

Uncle Jack's hand kept on moving over Jeannie's hair. David could see that he was thinking about what he had just been told. "I should have noticed that," he said finally. "I guess my leg was hurting a lot." Then a puzzled frown came back to his face. "Why didn't you tell me, David?"

David stared into the fire, avoiding his uncle's eyes.

Uncle Jack's voice went on. "Oh! I understand, David. There wasn't anything I could do about it anyway with this broken leg. Now what's this about a snow sign?"

David told him, "We tramped out a message in the snow on the lake so that the planes could see it when they flew over."

"David! That's wonderful." There was a lift in his uncle's voice. It held a note of respect which gave David a fleeting glow of warmth. "How did you think of such a clever idea?"

David turned around in the growing dusk, placing his back to the fire. "Yesterday, when we went to look at the other cabins, we saw tracks in the snow. Jeannie said I was reading the tracks when I told her what kind of animal had made them. Then last night I did some writing in the snow with the axe, and I thought if I could do that, we could write a big message on the lake by tramping out letters in the snow."

"David!" His uncle's voice was warm with admiration. "I think that's wonderful."

"But a plane came over, low down," David continued, "and it never came back."

"Yes, I heard it," said Unce Jack.

David saw the light fade from his uncle's eyes, and the harsh lines come back to his face. There was deep silence in the cabin; then Uncle Jack said, "Put some more wood on the fire, will you, David?"

"Uncle Jack, can't we have the radio on?" Jeannie was asking.

Uncle Jack hesitated as if he were about to say no. Then he reached for the radio as he saw Jeannie watching him. He turned the knob.

The radio came on, playing music softly in the

firelit cabin. The music continued for a short time, then was interrupted by a voice: "This is Logan Bates, bringing you your five o'clock up-to-the-minute news." There was a slight pause. "Storms lash the coast of Europe tonight in one of the worst gales of the season. . . ." Would he never get to the home news? They all moved a little with impatience. Finally it came: "Still no news of the three people who have been missing in a small plane over the Sierras. . . ."

Blackness and coldness came with a rush to David's heart. He did not realize until now that he had been hoping—hoping that somehow—Uncle Jack's words penetrated his dark thoughts. "It's time we had something to eat."

David looked at him. Uncle Jack seemed smaller, more discouraged since he'd been told about the plane under the trees and the other plane that had not seen the snow message. David went into the kitchen part of the cabin and pulled open the cupboard door. He counted the cans—one, two, three, four, five; that was all. Perhaps, he thought, there were other porcupines in the woods, but the thought of killing one made him feel a little sick.

"Up you get!" There was Uncle Jack's voice, speaking to Jeannie. "There's my girl! Now you go to the kitchen and see if you can help David get us something to eat."

David reached up for the can opener as he heard Jeannie come up behind him in the kitchen. "Guess what we've got for supper," he said, trying to cheer her up as he struggled to open the large can of baked beans.

"Let me, David." Jeannie took the can opener from him. "You get the kettle full of snow to melt."

David got the snow. It was quite dark outside now, and snowing heavily again tonight, although the wind wasn't blowing.

When the beans were hot, they ate them. There was stillness in the cabin except for the soft music on the radio. All at once Uncle Jack suggested, "Let's play I Spy." He looked once around the cabin, then said, "I spy with my little eye something that starts with *F*."

David took a big gulp of hot coffee. "*F*" he thought. This was a silly game when they weren't going to be rescued. Besides, he never was good at games which used sounds or words. "It might be *fire*," he thought, "or it could be *fireplace*." He did not say anything, and he did not look around the cabin.

"Furniture," Jeannie said.

"No," said Uncle Jack.

David could feel his uncle's eyes on him. "What do you think, David?"

"I don't know." How could Uncle Jack smile and play this silly game? Jeannie was looking around, her eyes beginning to smile. How could she forget where they were?

"Finger?" Jeannie said.

David carried the cups to the kitchen and put them in the sink. The game went on beside the fireplace, but David kept thinking of food. He had wanted more at dinner, but Uncle Jack had eaten very little; so he had not taken more. He thought of the way his mother fixed the turkey at Christmas—how it smelled, and how the golden brown skin stretched, and how it crackled when you bit into it.

The program on the radio had changed. It must be a funny one, David thought, because there was a lot of laughing. He could hear it above the voices of Uncle Jack and Jeannie.

The voices on the radio stopped and music began

again. Then after a song the announcer began, "When we come to the end of the year, the old songs are the best, so that we think back over the years. . . ."

"Celebrate the New Year," David thought. "Yes, it was close to New Year's. Maybe by New Year's they wouldn't even be—" He walked to the living-room part of the cabin and stood with his hands in his pockets, staring at the black window with the whispering snow behind it.

A quick, excited voice broke right into the radio program. "We interrupt this program to bring you a news flash. The three persons lost in the Sierras for the past three days have been found."

David stood rooted to the spot, his eyes still on the dark window. He did not breathe. Behind him he heard the small sharp sound of Uncle Jack spinning the radio volume control.

"Captain Anderson of the Pacific Air Command sighted what he believes to be a message from Jack Milton and the two children lost with him in the Milton plane."

"Uncle Jack!" Jeannie's head came up as David turned to them. "What is it?"

"Sh! Sh!" Uncle Jack sat tense in the bed, listening.

The radio continued, its phrases beating on David's ears while his mind tried to take in what he was hearing. He watched Uncle Jack.

"Just at dusk . . . low on gas . . . getting dark, so he could not go back . . . message read 'Help . . . all safe . . . Jack Milton.' An arrow pointed toward the shore."

"They saw it!" The words burst from David with a shout. He jumped as high as he could in the cabin and came down hard on his feet. "They saw the sign!"

"David!" Jeannie's eyes were shining as she sprang up with a rush and threw her arms around him in a wild hug.

The radio continued: "The signal must be recent. . . . Anderson reported it clearly visible even though snow fell heavily in the mountains last night."

"David, you did it!" That was Uncle Jack shouting from the bed. "Hurrah!" And he threw his pillow at them where they danced together round and round in the middle of the room.

"Here are the details," continued the radio voice.

They dropped, panting, beside the bed, still laughing while they listened.

"Anderson is not certain . . . believes the location to be either Silver Lake or Twin Lakes. . . . Both are in the locality where he searched this afternoon." Music began as the report ended.

Uncle Jack's eyes were shining. "David, there isn't one boy in fifty who would have thought to do what you did—and it worked!"

Uncle Jack was looking at him, not as a man looks at a boy, but as a man looks at a man. David felt his heart swelling up so that it seemed to fill his chest. "Jeannie helped," he said.

"How will they rescue us, Uncle Jack?" Jeannie was dancing again, round and round in the middle of the cabin, hugging the pillow that Uncle Jack had thrown at them.

"I don't know." Uncle Jack laughed, and David realized that he had not heard him laugh like that since the morning they left San Francisco. "But it can't come too soon for me."

The radio went on playing music, then repeating the announcement with slight changes. They heard little of it, for they were so excited that there were usually two of them talking at once, if not three. Their names came again: "Jack Milton . . . Jeannie Hamilton . . . David Hamilton. . . ."

Jeannie sang a little song to herself as she danced:

"We . . . 're going to . . . be rescued.
We . . . 're going to be rescued."

until finally she got so out of breath that she fell down in front of the fire, panting, still holding the pillow.

"Helicopter," said David. "That's how they'll rescue us." He threw more logs on the fire until it blazed up, filling the room with light.

"That's enough, David." Uncle Jack was holding his hand in front of his face to screen it from the heat. "Don't burn the place down before they rescue us."

The message came again: "It may be Silver Lake or Twin Lakes. Both are small lakes on Route 88 to Carson Pass." The announcer paused. "At the present time it has been impossible to contact Mr. or Mrs. Hamilton for comment, but . . ."

"Sh!" David hushed Jeannie's song. "That's Mother and Dad."

There was a deep stillness in the cabin as they all listened, but the announcer said nothing further. Jeannie began her song again. David walked up and down, taking giant strides to the door and back to the fireplace. He tried to make it in fewer steps each time.

Then the radio music was interrupted again: "A party of skiers, led by Sven Sorgaard, ski coach of Snow Line Lodge, has set out from the lodge up Route 88, to try to locate the crash victims. The party left at six o'clock. With snow conditions as they are, Sorgaard thinks they should reach Silver Lake by ten tonight. Sorgaard has announced that if nothing is found at Silver Lake the party will push on to Twin Lakes."

"But they'll find us here, won't they, Uncle Jack?" Jeannie held her pillow tightly to her as she sat on the floor, looking up at Uncle Jack.

"We'll make sure that they do," Uncle Jack said. "We'll light a fire on the lake so they can see it from the hills around the lake."

The radio came back with further word: "Snow is falling in the mountains and may increase during the night, so those in charge feel it is better to send in the ski party than to take a chance on being able to use a helicopter in the morning, with visibility zero, as it well may be by daylight. . . ."

David was struggling into his boots. A fire on the lake! This was something he could attend to. He was going to build the biggest, brightest, roaringest fire since— Why, oh why, did fingers feel all thumbs when he wanted to hurry?

"Wait for me!" Jeannie reached for her boots, too.

"Wait a minute, wait a minute!" Uncle Jack made his voice heard above the radio and Jeannie. "The ski party couldn't get here until ten at the earliest, and it's only seven now." Jeannie and David were suddenly quiet.

"But we have to plan," he went on to comfort them. "There's wood to get, and we'll have to make a big pot of coffee. Those men will be cold. It must be at least fifteen miles from Snow Line Lodge."

Jeannie had danced into the kitchen before the words were finished. "Come on, David," she called. "You get some snow to melt."

Never had time gone so slowly for David. It seemed as though each minute took an hour to pass. Jeannie and he boiled all the water the kettle would hold, and each time one of them looked at Uncle Jack, he said, "No, it's not time yet."

By eight o'clock the water had boiled and boiled. Eight-thirty—the slow minutes ticked away. The radio came on now and then with a repeat of the news about them. There was little added except that the radio stations had made contact with Mother and Dad, and they were standing by.

Nine o'clock! David kept looking out of the door until Uncle Jack complained that he was freezing them to death, and suggested they play I Spy. But even he could not seem to keep his mind on the game.

David wondered how grownups could seem to keep so cool and talk about little things. Perhaps Uncle Jack was just as excited as Jeannie and he were, but he'd learned not to show it.

It was nine-fifteen when Uncle Jack gave the signal to start. Then he glanced quickly at Jeannie, who was yawning, and said, "Suppose we let David light the fire on the lake and Jeannie keep the water boiling for coffee?"

David felt sorry, because Jeannie looked disappointed and he would have liked to have her out with him. It would be very lonely out on the lake at night. He thought that Jeannie was going to coax to go, but she just looked at Uncle Jack, her eyelids drooping over her eyes. Then she sighed and dropped her boots. "All right," she said.

Uncle Jack gave him careful directions. "About one hundred yards from here," he said. "Go off the end of the pier and ski out while you count a hundred strides."

"Sure, sure," David said. He was struggling into his jacket. He reached for his axe and for the door latch.

"Wait a minute, David." Uncle Jack called him back. "What are you going to use to light the fire?"

"Matches," David told him. Grownups could be so dense sometimes. "I'll come for them when I get the wood arranged for the fire."

"That's right," Uncle Jack agreed. "Get the wood out there first. But you won't be able to light a fire in this snow, not with matches, that is, even if it isn't windy."

"He's a Boy Scout." Jeannie defended David.

"You'll have to take a piece of burning wood from the fireplace," Uncle Jack said, "a piece with one end burning, so you can carry it by the other end." He pointed to a stick in the fireplace. "Then when you get out there, if it has stopped flaming, you can swing it around in the air so that the wind will make it flame again."

"Sure," David promised. "I'll come back for it when I get the wood ready." He opened the door, as he had so many times that evening, and looked into the rapidly falling snow.

"David!" He heard Uncle Jack's voice behind him. "You must never lose sight of the cabin window. We don't want you to get lost on the lake in the snowstorm."

David shut the door slowly and felt along the wall for his skis. He hoped that Uncle Jack was right about there being no big game around here. It would be easy for a bear to hide among these black shadows. For a moment he was afraid. Then he drove the thought from his mind and started for the woodpile.

With his arms full of wood, David skied down the pier and out onto the lake. He counted to one hundred; then he stopped and looked back. He could see the light from the cabin window, no bigger than a star. His teeth chattered as he stooped to lay the wood, crisscross on the snow. Then he went back for the burning piece of wood.

While he carefully carried it out of the cabin,

Jeannie held the door open. It smoked, and the smoke blew back into his eyes and down his throat, so that he coughed. He carried it to the wood he had piled ready for lighting; then he swung it round and round in the air until there was a shower of sparks in the night. Uncle Jack had been right; the wood burst into flames, and he thrust it into the waiting fuel.

The fire did not make as much light as he had thought it would. It lit up only a small part of the lake and made him realize how big and black the lake

and the night were. The snowflakes seemed to fall out of nowhere into the small circle of light around the fire. David brought more wood, and when the fire burned well, he went back into the cabin.

He stamped his feet on the cabin floor to get the snow off them. "It's going well," he announced to Uncle Jack.

But Uncle Jack was saying, "Sh— sh—" Then David saw that Jeannie was lying on her blanket. She had fallen asleep.

He tiptoed over to the fireplace.

"We'll let her sleep," Uncle Jack said. "She's tired and she'll be up when the rescue party gets here."

"The fire doesn't seem very big," David whispered. He stood before the fireplace in the quiet cabin, warming his hands and looking down at Jeannie. She looked smaller when she was asleep.

Uncle Jack smiled. "It's big enough," he whispered. "A fire can be seen for a long distance at night, even in a snowstorm."

David stood thinking about the events of the evening. Then—he did not know quite why or how it happened—suddenly he was spilling out something he felt he wanted Uncle Jack to know. "I can't read,

Uncle Jack." His voice came out in a hoarse whisper in the quiet cabin. Then he watched Uncle Jack's face. "Jeannie spelled all the words I put on the snow this afternoon, and she had to read the labels on the cans of food for me."

Uncle Jack did not look shocked. His voice was quiet and slow as he said, "Anyone who has done what you've done certainly could learn to read if he had someone to help him—and if he wanted to work hard at it—and if he wanted very much to learn to read." He was silent a minute. "Everyone has trouble with something. We can't always have things come easily, you know." He cleared his throat. David held his hands to the fire as he listened.

"You have trouble with reading; other people have trouble with other things," said Uncle Jack. The fire crackled. "But this I do know—there aren't fifty boys in the United States who would have thought through the problem you had here as you have done. And if you can't read, there are going to be a good many boys in your school who'll be proud to help you figure it out after this."

When David went back to the cold and the snow and the loneliness, Uncle Jack's words went with him.

They were very sweet, and he turned them over and over in his mind. "There aren't fifty boys in the United States—" He drove a doubled fist into his open hand. "When I get back to San Francisco," he said aloud, "I'm going to learn this time, so there!" He skied to the fire and put more wood on it.

As he stood watching the fire, a sudden noise made him lift his head. "What was that?" he asked himself. "It sounded like a shot." Then he saw the light. Even through the rapidly falling snow, even though he had never seen one before, he knew what it was—a signal shell, fired by someone on the hills at the head of the lake. It arched up into the blackness, shining in the night, a message from the rescue party. He realized they must have reached the hills at the head of the lake and were able to see his fire. He piled on more wood and more wood, higher and higher until the flames leapt upward.

He did not have to wait very long until he heard the voices of the approaching party, deep voices of men who moved along rapidly on their skis. He wanted to run to the cabin to waken Jeannie and to tell Uncle Jack too. But most of all he wanted to be the first to meet the men as they came forward out of the night, swinging along on their skis. So he stood where he was, wondering what he should say when they came. Their flashlights bobbed along in a line across the frozen lake. What should he say to them? He guessed that "Howdy" would be best. Yes, that would sound right. He stood quiet now, watching the bobbing flashlights come closer.

"Hello!" A shout from the men reached him.

David took a big breath and faced the oncoming men, their shapes dim in the falling snow. "Howdy!" he yelled.

CHAPTER EIGHT

Out of the Night

DAVID SKIED up the snow-covered pier beside Sven Sorgaard. Sven was the biggest man he had ever seen; in his ski parka he looked like a mountain. His great strides took him swiftly up the pier, while David puffed along beside him. Behind them came the man they called Elmer. David had noticed that he was much smaller than Sven, he moved quickly on his feet, and he talked a lot. The names of the last three men David had not heard. They were coming along behind Elmer. David was bursting to tell Sven and Elmer all about the crash, but he felt it would be childish to chatter; so he said nothing except, "My uncle, Jack Milton, has a broken leg."

"Well, what do you know?" Elmer whistled behind David. "So you made the signal in the snow? And you've been doing all the work since the crash?"

"Sure." David turned his head to talk to Elmer. "I did—" Then he remembered and stopped himself. He wasn't going to chatter.

"Where is the plane?" Elmer asked.

David's hand swept out in the darkness. "Over there, across the lake, under the trees," he said.

"Boy!" Elmer looked around him in the shadows at the rocks beside the pier. "What a place to crack up, boy!" He turned to the man behind him. "What do you say, Joe?"

"Yes, bad." The man behind Elmer must be named Joe. David had noticed at the fire that he was very tall and had very black eyes.

David opened the cabin door. "Here we are," he said. He stood back while Sven bent his head and stepped through the doorway. Elmer waved David on, so David went in next.

Uncle Jack was sitting up. "You know," he said, "I'm glad to see you fellows!"

Sven chuckled. "Bet you are, now." He seemed to fill the whole cabin, he was so big.

In fact, the cabin seemed full of men, David thought, as he sat down on Jeannie's bed. She was awake now and sitting up under her blanket, looking very sleepy and a little bit cross.

"Well!" Elmer whistled as he pulled a chair to the foot of Jeannie's bed. "A lady," he said, "and here I am with my old clothes on."

Jeannie smiled, then immediately thought of her duties as a hostess. "I'll get the coffee on," she said, struggling out from under her blanket.

"Sit still and get waked up first," Sven told her. He sat down on the end of Uncle Jack's bed while the rest of the men got out of their parkas. "Besides—" he winked at Jeannie— "Elmer, here, is the youngest man we have. Can't even grow a beard yet, but he's a good hand with a coffeepot. That's why we brought him."

"That I am, that I am," Elmer said. He went to the cookstove and raked the ashes, whistling all the time. His eyes swept the bare cupboards. "Looks like you folks were about out of food." The smile faded from his face; then it was back again. "We brought lots, though," he assured Jeannie and David.

At the thought of food David's stomach felt weak.

"Food?" Jeannie was wide awake in a minute. "What?" she asked.

"Beans," Elmer said. David saw the dismay on Jeannie's face and realized that his own must be showing the same disappointment. Elmer burst out laughing. "No," he said, "something better." He winked at Jeannie. "Come see," he coaxed.

David turned his attention to the men. It was wonderful to have the cabin so noisy, so full of people. Sven was sitting on the bed, talking to Uncle Jack about the broken leg. Joe, his black eyes and quiet face showing nothing of what he was thinking, sat in a chair, watching Uncle Jack and Sven. One man was turning the pages of a magazine. He was a big man, too, and looked a bit like Sven, but he was younger, and not quite so big as Sven.

"That's Gunnar."

David looked up to see who had spoken. His eyes met Joe's. There was no expression on Joe's face as he repeated, "That's Gunnar, Sven's brother."

"Oh," David said. "Thanks." He did not know quite what to do. How had Joe known that he wanted to know all their names?

"And I'm Harold." The last man was putting

wood on the fire as he turned to speak to David. He smiled. "Have you got us all straight now?"

"Yes, I guess so," David said, looking up at Harold.

"I used to be called Carrots," Harold said. He smoothed his bright red hair as he stood up.

The smell of food came from the kitchen—smells that David had not known in a long time. Elmer was frying bacon. Uncle Jack began to tell them about the crash. Sven and Harold got out pipes and filled them with tobacco as they listened. Gunnar looked up, listening, forgetting the magazine on his knees.

All these men looked competent, big, as if they could handle anything that came along. Suddenly David felt the weight of responsibility he had carried for the past few days slip from him like a great stone from his shoulders. There wasn't anything he had to do. There wasn't anything he had to plan. There were big strong men here. He didn't have to worry. These men would take care of everything.

"Gosh!" David said aloud. It had come to him, as he sat thinking and watching the men, that sometimes it was wonderful not to have to be grown-up. Growing up was what he had been doing the last few days. It meant taking care of others, trying to think

things out for them, and knowing you might make a mistake. He shook his head to clear it of the thoughts, and he smelled the bacon again. "I'm hungry," he said. He was very sleepy too.

"Come and get it!" Elmer brought the bacon, a huge platter of it, all crisp and brown, and a plate of bread piled high. There were cups of steaming coffee on the table. The last wisp of his responsibility slipped from David like a cloak, and he rushed to the table and sat down beside Jeannie, next to Elmer.

"Bread," David said. "Bread!" He took a piece and bit out a huge white circle, then let his tongue explore around it in his mouth. "Boy," he said, "bread's good, even without butter or jam, not toasted or anything. When you haven't tasted it for a long time, bread is about the best thing in the world, I guess." He took another huge bite; then he realized that the men were laughing at him.

Elmer was standing at his elbow with the platter in his hand. "Don't you want some bacon, David?"

He had no idea what time it was when he stopped eating bacon and bread. He had no idea how much he ate. He remembered clearly the taste of the bacon. He remembered being very sleepy, and the darkness of the night held back by the roaring fire, and the voices of the men as they talked. Dimly, through sleeping and waking, he knew that someone had put him on one of the beds and thrown a blanket over him.

Another time he knew that the men weren't going to sleep that night; they were sitting around the fire and drinking coffee. Then, again, he remembered something about the men changing the splints on Uncle Jack's leg. Through the waking and sleeping, he gathered the thread of the plans the men were making, plans to get them all back to the outside world tomorrow. He heard his own name mentioned more than once, and he knew that the night was wearing away, that the blackness of the window had become a grayness looking out into the coming dawn.

Then, for a time, he must have slept heavily, for the next thing he knew it was morning, and he came fully awake with the decision that had been forming during the long night—that for sure he had made up his mind about the future. He was going to be a skier like Sven, and probably live in Switzerland so that he could rescue people who were lost, and save them from avalanches. Yes, that was what he was going to do.

"About time!" Uncle Jack was smiling from the

other bed as he saw David's eyes open. "Thought you were going to sleep the clock around on us."

"What time is it?" David wanted to know.

"Eight." Uncle Jack looked at his wrist watch.

"And what day is it?" Jeannie had awakened, too, and was sitting up with her blanket held tight around her chin.

"The thirty-first of December," Elmer told her, "and you'd better get up, Jeannie. Got to get you back home today for sure, because I have a date tonight with my girl, for New Year's Eve in San Francisco."

Jeannie laughed. "I bet you don't have a girl."

David laughed, too. It was wonderful to wake up and find that someone had lit the fire and someone else had made breakfast. "I'm hungry," he said.

Sven looked at David with his eyebrows raised. "Seems to me those were the last words we heard out of you last night," he said. "Never saw such a hungry boy." He pointed to the table. "Breakfast's ready. Joe cooked it. Elmer is good for midnight snacks, but he isn't any good for cooking breakfast."

"Why not?" David asked. "If someone can cook bacon at night, can't he cook it in the morning?" Then he saw Uncle Jack laughing at him.

"Just before you two have breakfast, I think we'd better tell you about the plans for the day, David and Jeannie," Uncle Jack said. "Sven and the other men are going to take us out to Snow Line Lodge."

"Isn't a helicopter coming for us?" Jeannie asked.

"It's still snowing a little," Uncle Jack explained. "A helicopter might have a rough time getting over the mountains into this valley. Then it would have to come down under the fog and land in the deep snow on the lake. It might not even be able to find Silver Lake."

A sense of responsibility came back to David. "How will they get you out, Uncle Jack?"

"They will carry me out. They can carry you and Jeannie too, if you get tired of skiing. It isn't really very far—it's only down the lake up into the hills to Route 88, then just fifteen miles to Snow Line Lodge."

"Couldn't we get an airplane to come?" Jeannie insisted.

"'Fraid not, Jeannie." Uncle Jack shook his head. "No way to call for one, even if it were a good idea. They can carry me through the woods in a sling made of blankets, between two of the men." Uncle

Jack was showing them how with his hands. "See," he said, "it will go around the men's shoulders, so I can lie in it and they can walk one behind the other."

Jeannie looked doubtful. "And how will they carry me if I get tired?" she wanted to know.

"Pickaback!" Elmer said. "All the way if you like."

Sven interrupted. "It's still snowing, Mr. Milton, but not too much, and it's daylight now. I think these two should eat so we can get going."

David and Jeannie went to the breakfast table while Sven continued talking to Uncle Jack. "Joe will stay behind to see that the fire's out and that the windows and door are nailed up again. The rest of us will get started, and Joe will catch up."

David found the trip along the lake very different from the one he and Jeannie had made two days before, when they had been alone and Uncle Jack had been left in the cabin. His skis flew over the snow, and he kept right behind Sven. Jeannie skied behind David. He could hear her singing a little song to herself. Harold and Gunnar came behind Jeannie. They carried Uncle Jack between them in the blanket sling. Elmer came last, whistling all the time, pulling the sled David had made from the skis. They would have Uncle Jack ride on it, once they finally reached Route 88.

David looked back at the cabin. Joe was boarding up the windows as they had been when David first saw the cabin. It looked lonely, now that they were leaving it again.

"There's the cabin where we saw the porcupine!" Jeannie called out.

David turned to see it. Yes, there it was; they were coming abreast of it now. Boy, this was exciting, now that he had no weight of worry on his shoulders. He drew in his breath and yelled, just to hear the echo bounce back from the dark woods along the shore. This morning everything looked friendly. The trees were just trees; they weren't dark and frightening as they had been two days ago.

Joe caught up to them as they reached the end of the lake. He was carrying the rifle. He came up to take Gunnar's place in carrying Uncle Jack's sling, and Gunnar took the rifle and moved up to the front of the line, letting Sven drop back to take Harold's place. Harold dropped out of the line, puffing, his face almost as red as his hair. Then they began the hard work of climbing up and across the wooded hills to Route 88.

Gunnar moved up slowly, weaving among the pines, making a trail for the rest to follow. The men with the sling had slow going, and more than once had to come almost to a dead stop to get the sling around the dark pines. These stops were all that saved David.

They had crossed the lake at a fast pace for him, but he had decided that he was not going to be carried out to the ski lodge. He was going to ski every step of the way on his own two feet. But his breath was coming in gasps, and his legs were trembling long before they reached the top.

Jeannie had given up very soon. She rode now, pickaback on Elmer, shouting comments to Uncle Jack, David and the rest. Her feet were hanging down on either side of Elmer with her skis, which she still wore, sticking out under his arms in front and at the back. "Hi! David," she called. "I'm going to beat you to the top."

David could not have shouted back even if he had wanted to. "I'm going to—make this—if it's—the last– thing I—do!" he panted in whispers to himself as he staggered forward.

Harold was right behind him as he reached the top of the hill. "You're going to make a skier one of these days," he said.

"Everybody O.K.?" That was Gunnar at the head of the line.

"Let's get on with it!" Elmer shouted, and jumped up into the air on his skis, so that Jeannie squealed and would have fallen if she had not wrapped her arms around Elmer's head.

"Oh—oh, stop!" she cried.

At the top of the hill they all halted for a minute to rest. Sven took charge again. Passing his end of the sling to Gunnar, he inspected David's sled. "Nice job," he told David, "considering what you had to work with. Should do fine for Mr. Milton now we're on the road."

David watched the men lower his uncle slowly to the sled. He was thinking how hard it had been to get Uncle Jack onto the sled when they left the plane. He hoped he would be as strong as these men when he grew up. They lifted Uncle Jack as though he didn't weigh anything.

"Where's the road?" Jeannie was looking all around from her perch on Elmer's back.

"Right ahead of you," Elmer said, pointing. They saw that it was the long aisle through the dark trees stretching down the hills.

"I wouldn't have known it was a road," David said. "There aren't any tracks."

"Cars can't get up this way in winter," Sven said. "This Route 88 goes on to Carson Pass."

They moved off down the road in double file now, because the road made traveling easier.

At one o'clock they stopped for lunch. Sven cleared a little place in the snow at the side of the road, and Harold and Elmer rolled up a couple of logs for seats. Joe had pulled out a frying pan and a coffee pot from one of the packs, and Gunnar was making a fire. David watched. Gunnar picked out a piece of wood with bark on it, then stripped the bark with a quick stroke of his knife, reaching in for the paper-thin, brown inner bark, until he had a ball of it. He placed that on the ground, lit it, and as it burned, broke small twigs from a dry branch, adding them patiently twig by twig until he had a fire.

"That's the way I could have done it on the lake last night," David said to Uncle Jack.

"A smoldering stick such as you used is better, David," Uncle Jack said, "especially if it's windy."

Gunnar looked up. "Yes," he said. "This is best when you haven't a smoldering stick."

David made a sandwich for himself out of a slice of bread and hot bacon, and sat down on a log while he ate it. It would not be very long now before they would reach the ski lodge. Would there be reporters and camera men, waiting to take their pictures and interview them? He thought of scenes in the movies. What would he say when reporters asked him if he liked living in a cabin, lost from everyone else? He tried to think of a suitable answer.

When the bread and bacon were gone, the men smoked. Then Sven knocked out his pipe and stood up. "O.K., Mr. Milton?" he asked, looking at Uncle Jack.

"I'm fine; think I'll do all of my traveling this way hereafter." Uncle Jack's face was white and he looked tired, but he seemed happy today.

"How about you, David?"

With a shock David realized that Sven was asking him if he wanted to be carried. "I'm fine," he said firmly, "just fine." He did not want the reporters to see him coming in pickaback!

As they started off again, David sensed the excitement in the group. The lodge must be close now. The men had quickened their pace. They took turns carrying Jeannie and pulling Uncle Jack. David was tired, but he meant to ski to the lodge on his own two skis, and no one was going to help him. The way was longer than he thought, and his legs began to ache with the strain.

Sven must have noticed that he was tiring, for the leader slowed down a little. "Soon be there," he said. "Just a few more miles."

It seemed like a lot more than a few miles to David, but as he listened to the men and tried to swing along on his skis as they did, he forgot the ache in his legs. Up one hill they went and down another, under the low gray sky. Finally they topped a long rise, and David saw the lodge before Sven pointed it out.

"There!" Sven said. "See between those two clumps of trees. That's the lodge."

"Oh!" Jeannie said. "Perhaps Mother and Dad will be there."

David hadn't thought of that. Perhaps they would. There were cars around the lodge, and he knew that Mother and Dad would come up if they could get there. He forgot his tired legs. To see Dad and Mother seemed suddenly more important than seeing the reporters and the camera men. "Let's go," he shouted, driving ahead on his skis.

"Heads up," Joe called. "I'm going to fire a shot to let them know we're here." He raised the rifle, pointing it toward the sky. Jeannie covered her ears and closed her eyes.

David jumped when the rifle cracked, even though it did not sound as loud as he had thought it would. He heard the shot echo from the dark hills; then he saw someone wave from the lodge, then someone else. Next there was a crowd outside the door, and they were moving swiftly up the road on foot.

"David," Jeannie squealed, "there's a whole crowd to meet us."

David glided forward. Now, if only he could think of the right thing to say to the reporters— Then he saw his father, and he forgot reporters and everything else, except that he recognized Dad by his walk and the way he was hurrying toward the skiers.

David swallowed a lump in his throat and began to shout, "Dad! Dad!" It wasn't what he had planned, but he couldn't seem to help himself. "Dad, here we are," he called, and drove the skis on, forgetful of all else but the face of his father coming closer. "Dad!" Then he was there and he stopped, suddenly shy, as he realized that there were others all around,

staring at them. He stood, panting in the cold air, his legs shaking from fatigue, and raised his hand in a little salute. "Hi, Dad!"

A wave of sound and people rushed over him. In spite of the noise and confusion he learned that Mother had stayed at home to be near the phone and ready to start another search if the skiers had not found them, while Dad had driven up to the ski lodge to be near if the skiers did find them.

Jeannie was swept high into her father's arms, weeping, now that the strain was over. "Oh, Daddy," she sobbed, "I'm glad you've come. Poor Uncle Jack has a broken leg, and we hadn't anything to eat but beans, and David made a sled, and it was so snowy and we crashed." Then she threw her arms around her father's neck and buried her face in his collar and was quiet as he held her, stroking her head.

David watched the hand that stroked Jeannie, and then his father's face as he winked at his son.

"O.K., David?" his smile asked. And David, seeing the tired lines in his father's face, knew a little of the suffering of those at home, waiting for word of the lost ones. He thought of his mother. "I'm O.K.," he said. "We'd better get home to Mother, though."

"I've phoned your wife, Mr. Hamilton." It was one of the lodge attendants standing close to his father. I have her on the phone now, if you'd like to talk to her. I called her as soon as we knew that they were safe."

"Yes, they're safe." David noticed that his father only half listened. A warm smile flooded his face, and his hand reached out to hold David by the jacket, as though he had to feel him to make sure he was there. "Come on," he said. "Let's go talk to Mother."

It wasn't until after they had eaten hot soup at the lodge, until they were in the car and moving swiftly down the snowy road that David remembered there had been no reporters and no camera men to meet them. Uncle Jack was in another car ahead, all alone on the back seat with his leg stretched out. David felt very tired and sat back, listening as his father told of all that had happened from the time they were lost. Finally he asked, "Dad, why didn't they have a reporter or a camera man, to take our pictures when we got to the ski lodge?"

"Were you disappointed?" Dad asked, his eyes twinkling.

"No, but why didn't they, Dad?"

"There was a reporter there, David," his father explained. "He talked to me just before we got into the car. And there was a camera man. He took your pictures as you were coming up to us on your skis."

"No!" David couldn't believe it. "Will it be in the papers?"

"I guess so," Dad chuckled. "I don't much care now that I have you two back with me again."

"Why didn't the reporter talk to us?" Jeannie wanted to know.

"He knew you'd be very tired," their father explained. "Did you want to talk to him, David?"

"Oh!" David found it hard to put into words. "I guess not," he said.

"He's riding into the city with Uncle Jack," Dad continued, "talking to him now." Then he smiled at Jeannie and David where they sat beside him on the front seat of the car. "He's coming to talk to you this evening—" he paused to let that sink in— "if you don't mind."

"I'm going to tell him how David looked after us," Jeannie said, nodding her head to make her words important.

"And I'm going to tell him what a good cook Jeannie is," David said.

"And I'm going to tell him how proud I am of both of you and how nice it's going to be to have you around the house again," said Dad.

Night was falling as they reached San Francisco. David woke up to find that they were crossing the Bay Bridge, the car running smoothly under the fog lights, the other cars swishing past them on the smooth steel surface.

Jeannie sat up and shivered. "Where are we?" she asked.

"Bay Bridge," he said. "Mother will be waiting."

The car rushed across the bridge, turned right, and then headed for the west side, where they lived. In no time at all they drove up to the door. Mother must have been waiting there, because it was thrown wide long before the car had rolled to a stop. Mother came out with a rush, down the steps and along the walk, her arms out to them.

"Mother!" Jeannie was out of the car and flying for her mother's arms ahead of David. David saw that she was crying and that there were tears in his mother's eyes too.

"There, there!" Mother was patting Jeannie and holding her as she reached with her other arm for David. "Everything is all right now."

It was wonderful to be a small boy again for just a minute. Then David was striding down the hallway with Patty running to keep up. "Food!" David said. "I'm going to eat and eat and eat. . ." He caught the odor of baking from the kitchen. "Look out, apple pie!" he added. "Here I come!"

CDEFGHIJK 06987
PRINTED IN THE UNITED STATES OF AMERICA